URBANA FREE LIBRARY

3 1230 00433 3098

DISCARDED BY
URBANA FREE LIBRARY

URBANA FREE LIBRARY
(217-367-4057)

		DATE DUE	

D0966039

It was only eight-thirty. The staff of the clinic trickled in, most of them ignoring the demonstrators as they parked their cars and walked across the parking lot that widened in front of the building, their shoes slapping the puddles left by last night's storm. A few of them actually waved and smiled at the men and women gathered at the edge of the parking lot. Their bravado sparked off shouts and invective from Helen's companions.

"Baby killers! Don't you know that a woman's body is the temple of the Lord?"

"Millions of children, murdered every day! This must stop! It's a holocaust!"

"Dear Jesus, show them the error of their ways! Open their eyes, that they might see and praise God!"

Mimicking their behavior Helen moved her picket sign back and forth, careful to hold it high enough so as to avoid hitting anyone. She couldn't quite bring herself to say anything out loud, but so far her attendance at these protests and her quiet "prayers" seemed to satisfy the others that she was genuine. And no one had objected, so far, to her claim to be from out of town, gathering information on protest strategy for her own congregation. By stressing her awe and respect for Dr. Logan and his ministry, she'd paved the way with flattery and been accepted as one of their own.

Smoke and Mirrors

A Helen Black Mystery

Pat Welch

URBANA FREE LIBRARY

THE NAIAD PRESS, INC.
1996

Copyright © 1996 by Pat Welch

All rights reserved. No part of this book may be reproduced
or transmitted in any form or by any means, electronic or
mechanical, including photocopying, without permission in
writing from the publisher.

Printed in the United States of America on acid-free paper
First Edition

Editor: Christine Cassidy
Cover designer: Bonnie Liss (Phoenix Graphics)
Typesetter: Sandi Stancil

Library of Congress Cataloging-in-Publication Data

Welch, Pat, 1957 –
    Smoke and mirrors : a Helen Black mystery / by Pat Welch.
        p.   cm.
    ISBN 1-56280-143-0 (pbk.)
    1. Black, Helen (Fictitious character)—Fiction.
2. Lesbians—Fiction.   I. Title.
PS3573.E4543S6   1996
813'.54—dc20
                                                    96-26682
                                                        CIP

*This book is dedicated with
affection and gratitude
to the women of
Beyond The Fringe —
all of you know
how much you've done for me.*

Also — to RifRaf69, with all my love.

About the Author

Pat Welch grew up in small towns in the South until coming to northern California in 1976. She has lived and worked in the San Francisco Bay Area for ten years and currently makes her home in Oakland. *Smoke and Mirrors* is the fifth novel in the Helen Black mystery series.

Chapter One

Since mid-September, the rains had pummeled Northern California. And now, in late October, kids were thinking of Halloween — planning parties, putting together costumes, mapping out the best places for soaping windows and toilet-papering trees. Sunday night in Lafayette turned cold, damp and dark. The rain kept coming, in spite of the hopeful predictions of an assortment of meteorologists. Children all over the San Francisco Bay Area held their collective breaths and hoped for the promised clear weather that assured them of their tidal waves

1

of candy. In this bedroom town thirty minutes away from what the residents called "the City," as if San Francisco were a fabled land like Oz, wind and water howled and slew around the quaintly named streets and boxy tract homes, rippling the surface of swimming pools and demolishing the paper pumpkins and crepe witches festooned throughout the quiet neighborhoods.

While most of Lafayette's citizens slept in their beds, costumes ready for the following week and sacks of sweets tucked away in cabinets out of the reach of little hands, a few nameless, faceless people gathered in the rain outside a building on the outskirts of town. Lightning, a rare event in this part of California, etched a ragged slash across the face of the building, highlighting the words "LINVILLE MEMORIAL CLINIC" engraved in the old weathered stone. Formerly used as a meeting hall for a now-defunct men's club similar to Elks and Moose orders throughout the country, the clinic had opened its doors almost thirty years ago. Despite the good intentions of Ida Linville, an awe-inspiring matriarch of one of Lafayette's oldest and richest families — the kind that never seems to die off, somehow — the clinic was the bane of the small town's existence. Perhaps the mayor and town council had, in those days of hope and contentment in the early sixties, had a vision of patients coming and going from the Linville, clean and white and virginal, already blooming with health and happiness. A regrettable cold, or an elderly maiden aunt's bout with some slow wasting disease, maybe even a few broken limbs to bind — that was all they saw in the clinic's future.

Perhaps. Three decades were all it took to wipe

away that fond dream. Three decades later, the clinic, crumbling at the edges and constantly crying out for money,might be compared to the way Ellis Island looked around the turn of the century. At least, that's the way it was described by a lot of the people in town. Nestled in a shallow verdant basin near the Lafayette BART station, where rapid transit trains flew back and forth in metallic gleaming splendor over the Berkeley hills and under the bay to "the City," the clinic grounds were blessed with old-growth trees and lush foliage. A rambling stream, swollen now from all the rain, meandered through tall grasses behind the building. Wildflowers, almost developed out of existence by frenzied real estate lords, still bent and waved in the acre of land between the BART station and the clinic. In the spring, butterflies would weave delicate paths of color between stream and grass.

It wasn't the place so much as the people there. That's how everyone put it — all those quiet well-behaved voices describing the "deserving" and the "undeserving" poor. That natural beauty was wasted on people like that, they said. They should have razed the place long ago and made it a playground, or maybe another parking lot for BART, they said. Of course, the Linville family couldn't help it — the whole clinic project was tied up legally, no doubt, with all kinds of lawyers and accountants and trust agreements involved. And if the people of Lafayette knew anything, they knew what it was like to have someone's will tangled up in court. Maybe it was a tax write-off.

Regardless, people came. People with darker skins, unrecognizable languages and different food. People who couldn't afford to go to the suburban hospitals. People with no insurance. People with — imagine! — no bank accounts. And those children! Every time you looked around there was another family walking around, dirty and smelly and confused, asking where the clinic was. You were afraid to let your children out, sometimes, not knowing what they might see there.

Lafayette gritted its well-capped teeth and watched the clinic with a baleful eye. Disgusted by the constant panorama of the Bay Area's indigent population trooping to their town for inexpensive medical services, the angry residents waited to pounce on the first misstep, the first evidence of something that could be used to shut the damned place down.

Nothing really good, really juicy, popped up until the early 1990s, when abortion clinics and doctors who performed abortions were making headlines around the country. Although the good citizens refused, in general, to align themselves with such vulgar born-again types, the pro-life demonstrations outside the Linville seemed, at the very least, a good place to begin. Of course, they'd say, I'm all for a woman's right to choose. Don't get me wrong. It's just that the clinic is — well, it's not safe to have a place like that here in town. I mean, after all, the kinds of people a place like that attracts! There's bound to be trouble. I think the clinic should close. Or move, maybe. Out to a section that really needs it, further east.

Then there were shootings of doctors and bombings of clinics and violent demonstrations around the country. And Lafayette became more and more

4

afraid. And people kept on coming, in spite of everything.

So it was no real surprise to anyone when the vandalism started at the end of the previous summer. After the first wave of broken windows, fires started in the parking lot and curses sprayed in bright red paint across the walls of the clinic, even the small group that supported the Linville quieted down. These people, fearful for the town and their children, learned to swallow their protests or couch them in passive and harmless language. Nothing good could come from it now, they reasoned.

And even the security guards hired by the clinic's executive committee didn't seem to help at all. The Linville couldn't afford a guard around the clock, and what with all the protesters and pro-life demonstrations it seemed better to focus on security during the day when patients were coming and going. The expensive alarm system worked well, but the local police never seemed to get to the building in time, once an alert had flagged on, to catch whoever was doing these things.

Ugly things, too. Not just paint and fires and garbage, including the dead bodies of small animals. The worst part was yet to come, that very Sunday night.

Anyone watching the gathering outside the Linville that night would be hard put to tell how many people were there, or how old or what gender. It was just too dark and rainy. The wind whipped tree branches around the dim street lamps that dotted the parking area, giving the scene a strobe-light effect and muffling the conversation.

"C'mon, you fuckhead, don't drop it!"

"Jesus fucking Christ, you wanna get us caught?"

"Hey, chill, no problem. I got it." A brief scuffle as the group made it over the ineffectual chain-link fence was followed by the slap of sneakers on wet asphalt.

"Where did he go?"

"Here. My jacket got caught."

"Right, right. Asshole! Don't get left behind."

The only sound now was the thick gurgle of liquid flowing. The nauseating scent of kerosene caught on the rain and left oily traces in the cold air.

"God, that shit stinks. Don't drown it, okay?"

"What, you wanna do this right, or what? No pain, no gain, fuckhead." Several pairs of hands grabbed the gas-soaked rags from the heap on the asphalt. Some were carelessly flung at the clinic, slapping against the stone walls. A few were placed with great care along the front walkway, partially sheltered from rain by wide handrails.

"You sure this'll work with all this rain?"

"Look, have I fucked up yet? Just shut up and keep your shitty comments to yourself, all right?"

These words were accompanied by a strange rattling sound. Lightning flared briefly, gleaming off the can of spray paint that moved back and forth, back and forth.

"Come on, let's do it!"

Like a battle cry, the tense whisper galvanized the group into action. The paint ran and dripped a bit in the rain, but the storm was already dying out. The thunder moved away, westward towards the Berkeley hills, as the work continued. Wind ruffled the edges of the rags along the front of the clinic, and the stench of gas lifted up into the clearing sky.

"Shit, look!" Everyone turned east, looking away from the clinic. Over the rapid-transit track that stretched above the Linville into the heart of Lafayette, the sky, still turgid with clouds, paled into gray limned with streaks of pink and red. Sunrise was minutes away. The stream of cars flowing along the freeway to their right had thickened, slowed to a crawl, clogged with an ever-increasing caravan of commuters. Parallel to the freeway, the narrow BART station filled with anxious men and women, checking watches and staring eastward, straining for a glimpse of the train that would take them to work. "We gotta get the hell outta here!"

"Okay, let's get the rest of this shit done. That alarm is gonna go off any second now." A duffel bag was handed up and strangely shaped pieces handed around. Again the spray can hissed as everyone had a turn at coating what they held with the bright red paint.

"Fuck!" They weren't finished when the gong alarm boomed out into the night, shattering the silence. With desperate haste the group separated, tossing painted pieces around them in a scattered pattern that lined the front walk and the edges of the parking lot. One figure stayed behind, despite the piercing clang, arranging the things the others had dropped or thrown in panic. Fumbling in haste, the rags closest to the entrance flared up as the lighter touched them. At first the soaked cloth threatened to smoke and sizzle out in the damp, then the flame

7

took. A small fire burned, growing in fits and starts as it caught another rag in a burst of wind, spreading to a whole row of flame.

The lone figure finally left when the flashing red and blue lights of the local police poured up from the main road of Lafayette and into the parking lot of the clinic.

If they'd arrived moments earlier, the police would have seen a solitary someone running around the side of the clinic. Under the cover of darkness — which was fading fast as dawn crept closer — the figure ran through tall wet grasses behind the building and disappeared along the bank of the creek. By the time officers in uniform straggled through the tangle of weeds and grass, the iron gray sky threatened rain again.

"Anything?"

"Nothing. Again." The young police officer, so new that his uniform still creaked, sighed heavily and slipped around on the wet grass. "I think he ran around here and took off through the creek. See the mud here?"

His colleague, older and slower, crouched down and hunched against the cold wind. "Shit. Won't be able to get a lift off of this mess. Too much mud shoved all to fuck."

"They're just too quick. We can't seem to get a line on them. C'mon, let's get this sealed off."

By the time the two men had made their way back to the front of the clinic, the slender thread of sunshine had increased. Last night's work lay spread before them.

The fire hadn't done much damage beyond some

8

easily cleaned smudges on the old stone façade of the building. The graffiti were much worse, though — huge block letters in a crazy pattern of obscenities that stretched across the windows and doors, blazing out a message of hate.

"Ah, Christ!" The younger officer grimaced in disgust, while his older companion just shook his head. "I can't believe it. Who'd do a sick thing like this?"

"Some people think what goes on at this clinic is sick, too, you know."

"Hey, you don't think these pro-lifers are doing good here, do you?"

"Never mind what I think. Speaking of pro-lifers, those picket signs and holy rollers will be here soon. Better seal it all off."

His colleague nodded and went about his work, trying not to look at the splayed limbs and cracked heads all around him. It was the red paint that got to him most — the way someone had taken parts of plastic baby dolls and literally dipped them into what looked like real blood. His mind wanted to put the parts together and he struggled against the urge to gather the broken bloodied arms and legs together, to cradle and somehow heal them.

"This makes, what, the third time so far?"

"Right. Twice in the last few weeks, now this." The murmur of people starting their day grew louder, and the main street of Lafayette, just beyond a row of eucalyptus trees that lined the parking lot, was coming to life. The wheels of the day turned slowly, quietly, gathering speed with the passing minutes. "Yep, there's the whole gang now."

"Huh?"

"God's own little set of demonstrators."

Sure enough, the edges of picket signs poked through the row of trees. They were already here.

Chapter Two

Helen looked up into the gray October sky. She was certain the rain would start soon. Adjusting the picket sign in her hands, she glanced at her fellow pro-life demonstrators. One or two grimaced at the cold wind and splatters of raindrops, but most of them gazed at the front of the clinic, rapt, dedicated, serene in the knowledge that they were doing God's work.

Like the young woman next to her. Helen struggled to recall her name, finally met with success — Dawn? No, Donna. Her wide, vague blue eyes were closed tight, her face screwed up in a grimace, her lips moving in silent prayer. Donna had been born and raised in Lafayette, lived here all her life, and couldn't imagine why on earth any poor sinner would want to destroy a beautiful baby, God's gift of life. The only place Donna had ever seen people like those who came to the clinic was on television, usually the news, which portrayed the poor as drug-ridden, crime-infested, filthy and furtive. Donna was engaged to an upstanding young member of her congregation and she planned to have many babies and never have a job that would take her away from her family. "It's what God wants, Helen. It says so, right in Holy Scripture."

Suddenly the eyes flashed open and with a cute toss of her blonde hair, she turned to smile at Helen. "Oh, isn't this just — just so neat!" she said, her cheeks round and pink in the cold. "To know we're out here doing God's work! Praise the Lord!"

Helen smiled, nodded, closed her own eyes and bowed her head in a mimicry of prayer that hid her expression. Silently she amended Donna's words — Helen told herself she was doing the work of the Goddess by standing here, day after day, with all these fanatics, hoping to get a lead on the vandalism taking place at the Linville. If only Donna knew who and what she really was — Helen Black, Private Investigator from Berkeley, Lesbian Extraordinaire. Well, maybe not the last part. These days, Helen wasn't feeling too extraordinary.

Helen waited to lift her head until she heard Donna praying again. She didn't want to talk, she wanted to look. She scanned the small knot of people again. Unlike the men and women who straggled into the clinic every day, her colleagues in the Lord were all white, well-fed and prosperous. Helen wondered how many of them knew what it was like to go hungry, or lose a job, or even not take a vacation to Disneyland twice a year.

Helen sighed. That wasn't really fair. One thing her police work and her career as a detective had taught her was that one never knew, never, what was going on under the surface of any human being's life. As an outsider, Helen couldn't imagine the private struggles any of these people had, including little Donna, bundled into her padded pink parka.

Helen started when Donna dropped to her knees on the damp asphalt. Several other people did the same. Refusing to follow suit — the last thing she needed right now was a cold — Helen listened as a small, thin man at the head of the group led them in prayer.

Dr. Logan's height was no indication of his charisma. With outstretched arms, he stood, rigid, his feet planted like deep roots in the pattern of Jesus crucified, his voice loud and deep enough to carry across the band of followers as well as throughout the parking lot in front of the clinic.

"Dear Father in Heaven," he began, "look down on us, your humble servants, here doing your will." Murmurs of assent, a few soft "amens," and a ripple of people settled into prayer mode. "We ask your forgiveness for these poor young women, for they know not what they do! We ask you to bless our endeavors, to show your mercy and your glory to all your servants, here and everywhere!"

The murmuring grew louder, and Helen stiffened herself against the familiar feelings of anger and discomfort. It wasn't anyone's fault that she'd grown up in a small town in Mississippi, her daily life constrained and made miserable by religious people like those all around her right now. It wasn't anyone's fault that her own fundamentalist upbringing left her scarred and cautious of any sort of religious display. The constant barrage of righteousness, however, that she was faced with for the course of this investigation set her teeth on edge. Except for the lack of Southern accents, these people looked and acted just like the friends and family she'd grown up with — the same people who had overwhelmingly rejected her when her father kicked her out as a teenager because she was queer.

"Help these people to see the light, Lord, to see that what they do here is murder! Help us to show them Your way, Your truth, and Your light!"

"Amen, brother!"

"Praise God!"

"We love you, Jesus, we praise you, Jesus . . ."

The cries turned into strange, exotic-sounding chants as some of them started to speak in tongues. Those stricken by the Spirit babbled in varying pitches of unintelligible sing-song, their bodies weaving back and forth ecstatically to some rhythm that only they could hear. Helen gripped her sign and bowed her head again. This was the part she hated most.

It was only eight-thirty. The staff of the clinic trickled in, most of them ignoring the demonstrators as they parked their cars and walked across the parking lot that widened in front of the building, their shoes slapping the puddles left by last night's storm. A few of them actually waved and smiled at the men and women gathered at the edge of the parking lot. Their bravado sparked off shouts and invective from Helen's companions.

"Baby killers! Don't you know that a woman's body is the temple of the Lord?"

"Millions of children, murdered every day! This must stop! It's a holocaust!"

"Dear Jesus, show them the error of their ways! Open their eyes, that they might see and praise God!"

Mimicking their behavior Helen moved her picket sign back and forth, careful to hold it high enough so as to avoid hitting anyone. She couldn't quite bring herself to say anything out loud, but so far her attendance at these protests and her quiet "prayers" seemed to satisfy the others that she was genuine. And no one had objected, so far, to her claim to be from out of town, gathering information on protest strategy for her own congregation. By stressing her awe and respect for Dr. Logan and his ministry, she'd paved the way with flattery and been accepted as one of their own.

Helen watched as Bud Griffin, the burly security guard, opened the front entrance for the staff. Bright red paint, smudges from fires and a heavy security gate now marred what was once the graceful faux marble façade of the Linville. The fluted white pillars and Southern-style veranda were most likely permanently damaged by the graffiti and smoke. The clinic, Helen knew, certainly didn't have the money to restore the building — any spare funds had been used to put in the expensive alarm system that spread an ugly web across all the doors and windows.

Lights came on inside the building, and Helen felt

a brief spasm of regret that she couldn't be inside the warm, well-lit building. As if picking up a part of her thoughts, Donna said, "Sad, isn't it, that such a lovely building is used for Satan's work?"

"I wonder," Helen mused, "what old Ida Linville would say if she could see all this today? Us, I mean. The vandalism."

Donna shuddered. "Oh, don't even talk about that! Everyone is saying we're doing it, can you believe it?" She studied the building, and her eyes went vague again. "I'm sure Mrs. Linville wouldn't have wanted baby-murders happening here. I mean, I know the land is tied up in the Linville Trust, but Dave Linville ought to be able to stop the clinic from operating here, shouldn't he?"

Helen turned to listen, interested at this sudden and unusual comment. No one in the pro-life group had ever talked about Dave Linville and the Linville Trust before. "What do you mean, Donna?"

"Well, he is on the Executive Board, right? Isn't he in charge of things here?"

"He would have to answer to a whole bunch of people for his actions, Donna. Especially if the trust was set up to fund the clinic and carry out Mrs. Linville's wishes. And I guess her wishes were to keep the clinic up and running."

Donna snorted, wrinkling her pert nose in disgust. "Those are the laws of Caesar, Helen, not the Holy Word of God! That trust thing is the work of the devil, and Dave Linville will have to answer to the Lord for his sins!"

Helen sighed. She didn't know enough about the legal situation herself to comment, but she was certain that Caesar and his ilk were simply carrying out their legal duties. Rumor had it that Mrs. Linville's own daughter — the late aunt of Dave Linville, the current ruling scion of the family — had died from a botched abortion the year before the clinic opened.

It was almost nine. Soon the clinic's first patients would arrive. The demonstrators had subsided, resting and talking quietly among themselves, waiting for the first wave of people. Helen surveyed the crowd, wondering how they'd react if they knew she'd been hired by that same Executive Committee Donna had just mentioned to watch them, actually infiltrate them, in hopes of stopping the vandalism. The eager white faces that gazed out like a bank of pale flowers at the parking lot told her nothing. What was really going on inside? Which ones among them — if any — were responsible for the damage etched vividly on the old stone?

Dr. Logan turned to face them, glancing down at his watch. A sudden burst of sunshine broke through the black clouds overhead, catching the dull gleam of his bald pate and reflecting off of his spectacles. Age spots dotted his wrinkled hands. He passed out packs of leaflets to a select few.

"All right, folks," he intoned. "Doug and Marion, you take your people out by the entrances to the parking lot" — he waved at four couples, two for each end — "and hand these out. Mrs. Logan and I will stand by the front with ours." He beckoned to a plump matron with artificially bright red hair, who beamed and took the proffered brochures then trotted across the parking lot like a pigeon cooing its way to bread crumbs. "And the rest of you keep praying and talking to these people, letting them know God's love and glory! We'll whup the devil right here in his own front yard!"

Donna sighed deeply as the gathering broke up with cheers and applause. "Dr. Logan is just great! I can't believe how he's pulled this congregation together!"

Helen smiled. "He certainly has charisma."

"You know, Helen, maybe he could go to your church and give a talk. It's too bad their work is backsliding these days. We have to edify each other, support each other, you know?"

Helen nodded, murmured an agreement. At the moment, she was distracted from Donna's chatter by the arrival of a familiar car in the parking lot. The battered green Honda Civic had seen better days, and it sputtered and coughed into a space with a final death rattle. For what felt like the millionth time Helen watched the woman who got out of the driver's seat. Day in and day out, for two weeks, Helen had watched her bring frightened girls into the clinic, clearly fighting off her own fears each time.

Another woman got out of the car. "Allison, these people — I'm scared —"

"Don't worry, honey. That's why I'm here with you. There's nothing they can do." Allison strolled around the car with a defiant glance at the pro-life demonstrators, put an arm around her charge's shoulders and walked her across the parking lot to the entrance. The woman leaned close to the girl, whispering encouragement. Allison's thick black hair, cut shoulder length and streaked heavily with gray, set off her deep green eyes that flashed angrily at Dr. and Mrs. Logan, who thrust their pamphlets at the girl. Helen couldn't hear their conversation over the shouts and cries of the people around her, but obviously it wasn't a happy one. Allison's lean frame, much too thin for the baggy clothes she wore, tensed with fury at whatever the good doctor was saying, and after gently urging the girl inside the clinic she faced off with the surprised couple.

Whatever it was she said to Dr. Logan, he flinched and clutched his Bible close to his chest. Mrs. Logan blushed nearly as red as her hair and turned away in horror. Helen suppressed a smile, wishing she could have edged close enough to hear what the thin, furious, beautiful woman had said to them. After silencing the pair, Allison marched past Bud with a smile for the aging guard, then disappeared into the clinic.

Allison. This was the first time Helen had heard her name. What was her last name? Was there any way to find out? She couldn't risk it now, of course, but maybe later, when she met with the board to give her report, she could find out.

Another stray beam of sunlight bounced her reflection off the windows of a passing car. Helen had a quick look at herself — short, square-bodied, with blunt-cut short hair and deep-set dark eyes that stared back blankly. Huddled in her old down parka, grimly holding the sign with both hands, she certainly didn't present a friendly picture. Who was she kidding? Allison was probably married, with kids and a sensitive New Age husband who was in touch with his feelings.

Besides, Helen sighed, she had a job to do. Things were getting more exciting now. Along with the steady flow of cars pulling up to the Linville, small troops of people on foot were splashing through the parking lot, fixing their eyes on Bud in his blue shirt that stretched tight over a hanging belly. His bulldog features and gruff voice, not to mention the sidearm he carried, must have seemed like a beacon of safety for them. And so many of them, Helen knew, weren't coming to the clinic for abortions. She saw broken limbs, bandaged heads, heard coughs and sniffles and crying babies, and spotted several people who were probably on the clinic's methadone program.

But all Helen's colleagues in Christ could see were images of aborted fetuses swimming in blood and refuse. Their cries and prayers gradually took on harsher tones and soon the yelling started.

"Murderers! Murderers! God will fry you in hell!"

"Go fuck yourself, cunt!"

"You will pay the price! The Lord is my shepherd . . ."

"Yeah, well, tell the Lord to pay my fucking rent, you son of a bitch."

Many of the targets of their shouting couldn't understand English, anyway. They blundered, carrying babies and blankets, toward the clinic with furtive glances all around, whispering to each other in a variety of languages from around the world.

The shouters, though vocal, didn't make up the majority of demonstrators. For the most part the group murmured prayers, beseeching people with outstretched arms and faces strained with concern. Helen studied them as closely as possible, trying to picture any one of them lighting a kerosene-soaked rag or wielding a can of spray paint, their faces lit only by the dull gleam of the moon.

"Allison." It was only a whisper. At first Helen

wasn't sure she'd really heard it — maybe she'd only thought it. Then, again, "Allison."

Slowly, not wanting to draw attention to herself, Helen turned in the direction of the soft voice.

He stood at the very edge of the protesters, his hands empty of picket sign or leaflets, hanging by his side instead of folded in prayer. Heavy set and muscular, with that odd loose quality that age and misuse rendered on athletic male bodies, the man wore only a light windbreaker, unzipped and flapping open in the breeze, over his jeans and T-shirt. Several days' growth of beard grizzled his face, and his hair, slick and dirty blonde, probably hadn't been washed for a while. Helen watched as he clenched and unclenched his grimy fists, his gaze fixed and smoldering on the entrance of the Linville.

The rain began again, eliciting cries of dismay from Helen's companions. She pulled the hood of her parka up, realizing it would be a short morning for her. When she turned around again, the man was gone.

Chapter Three

"Allison? Let's see — oh, yeah. Her last name is Young. Yeah, I'm pretty sure that's right."

Helen accepted the drink offered by Dr. Jill Mason and leaned back into the overstuffed chair by the roaring fire to enjoy it all — the rain outside, a blazing fire inside, good liquor, and to top it all off the aroma of fresh baked bread. Helen had to admit, Frieda had done pretty well for herself with her new lover.

Not that Helen and Frieda hadn't had a comfortable home during the years they lived together. And Frieda had never been one to notice material possessions anyway — she'd been too busy, was busy still, making a name for herself as an artist. And she certainly seemed happy here, ensconced in the hills between Lafayette and Berkeley in an enormous house that took in a view stretching all the way across the bay to the Golden Gate Bridge.

"Why did you want to know?"

Helen was jerked abruptly out of her brooding. She told Jill about the scene she'd witnessed this morning between Allison and the Logans. "I was impressed with her style," she said.

Jill laughed. "I'm sorry I missed it." She eased her burly frame onto the cushions near the hearth and sat cross-legged, sipping her drink. The doctor's weight was solid, packed muscle that rested comfortably on her tall body, sure of its power and ability. That, more than anything else, Helen decided, was what made her so attractive — not the rather ordinary dull brown hair or the mud-brown eyes or her crooked smile — it was her confidence. Helen was still trying to dislike her ex-lover's new partner, but it was not an easy task. Why the hell couldn't Jill be a mean bitch, instead of a nice, intelligent, sensitive woman? And a doctor, too?

Frieda emerged from the kitchen carrying a wooden tray loaded with cubes of freshly baked bread and slices of various cheeses. "How's this?" she asked. "Do you think it's enough?"

"Oh, that's really great, Frieda." Jill stood up to help her and they took the tray to a long parson's table against the wall by the bay window. "No one is expecting dinner — this is strictly business."

Frieda smiled as she came back to sit next to Helen on the floor by the fire. "There, I've done my Ozzie and Harriet thing for the day. Can I be Frieda Lawrence, world famous artist, again?"

"Fine by me." Helen tried to smile as Jill leaned down to kiss Frieda on the cheek. It was a small, harmless gesture of affection, but Helen still felt a pang at their happiness. She cleared her throat and said, "So why is the Executive Board meeting here, Jill? Seems odd to do this in someone's house."

Jill shrugged. "Dolores — that's Dolores Wayne, the director — she thought it would be nice to get everyone away from the tensions of the workplace, with all the shit going on at the clinic."

Frieda snorted. "Meaning she wants to be able to have free-flowing alcohol."

"She's okay, really — just been behind a desk too long. I wouldn't be working at the clinic if it wasn't for her." Jill smiled.

Helen recalled Dolores Wayne as a nervous woman, full of giggles, dressed in a horrible flowered dress that only served to highlight her dead-looking skin and badly colored hair. She'd left the room several times to smoke while Helen was being briefed by the board on her investigation.

"What do you mean, she got you into the clinic?" Helen asked.

"Well, Dolores has been on the medical scene for years. You know, she actually got her doctorate in nursing? After going on the twenty-year plan to finish school? But she seems to be more comfortable behind a desk, away from messy patients. I think she's been in administration ever since she got out of school. Anyway, she knew I was looking for a place to do some real work, not just worry about whether or not I'd be getting a Jaguar or a Porsche next year."

Helen looked around the room, noticing the paintings and tapestries on the walls, the rich furniture, antique rugs, the incredible view. It was difficult to see any sacrifices Jill might have made, and Helen allowed a faint surge of outrage to slither into her thoughts.

"I know, I know. This place is not exactly a dump, right?"

"You could say that." Helen was careful to keep her voice neutral and her eyes away from Jill. Frieda, Helen noticed, sat very quietly, playing with the fringe on the nearest cushion. "Not bad at all, in fact."

Jill sighed and ran a freckled hand through her pale red hair. "It's true, my first few years out of medical school, all I thought about was finally, *finally* being able to do some real good. That's why I went to Central America." She got up and wandered over to the window. A few drops of rain spattered on the glass but the wind had blown most of the clouds away, and the Golden Gate sparkled like a necklace across the cold black water. Jill picked up a small box that rested on the window ledge and toyed with it, then tossed it over to Helen. "Here, look at this."

Curious, Helen opened the small enameled box. The light from the fire glowed on the red velvet lining. Helen slowly lifted the bullet out of its plush container and felt its weight in her palm. It had obviously been fired — the tip was blunted and the bottom looked as though it had been chewed by fine delicate teeth.

"That was taken from my leg fifteen years ago. It happened right before I left El Salvador with the rest of the medical team. A couple of the nurses — well, they didn't make it." Jill broke off for a moment and stared into the fire. When she spoke again, it was so softly that Helen had to strain to make out the words. "After that, I knew I had to just get the hell out, get on with my life, start living like a normal person again. You know — dogs, house with a yard, the works." Her voice grew louder, with undertones of amusement. "No more packages of noodles, five for a dollar. No more begging the landlord to let me be late with the rent. Nor more going to Mother and Father for another handout, embarrassing them with my perversions and my publicity."

Helen found herself watching Frieda, who still sat very quietly near the fire, carefully not looking at either herself or Jill. What was going through her mind right now?

"But that's all behind me now. Water under the proverbial bridge, as they say." Helen put the box into Jill's outstretched hand. Jill juggled it around as if it were a toy before placing it back in its position of honor.

"Now I'm fairly tame. All I do is volunteer at a clinic. Quite respectable!" Jill laughed aloud, inviting Frieda with her eyes to join her in the joke. Helen wondered who the performance was for — her or Frieda? Maybe just for Jill herself. Jill seemed a bit too eager to proclaim her blameless existence. And was that a note of regret Helen had heard in Jill's description of her brush with death? From her own experience with police work Helen knew the rush that could come with defeating mortality.

And Frieda, sitting so demurely, drinking it all in — did she really believe that? After living with Helen and arguing endlessly about the danger inherent in Helen's chosen career?

The doorbell softly sounded and Helen turned around as the nighttime chill swept over her.

"Jill, Frieda, how are you?" Dave Linville, patriarch of the Linville family, strode into the room. His heavy Western boots — Helen had never seen him without them — clumped heavily on the polished wood floor. "Good to see you, Helen." He pumped her arm vigorously in a manly handshake. In fact, everything about him was very male, from his wool plaid shirt to his aftershave. Difficult as it was to accept that Dick Tracy jawbone as the real thing, Helen never was able to pigeonhole him as a caricature. It was all genuine. The only question left was just how much those Levi's cost.

Next to enter was Carmen Espinoza, secretary to Dolores Wayne who generally took notes at the meetings. Her wild mane of black hair shone richly against the tight blue dress that stretched across her ample figure. Her heavy makeup gleamed in the firelight, and long nails like blood red spikes flitted over the bread and cheese, piling a small hill of food on a paper plate.

"If you gonna be mad at me 'cause I'm late you have to tell my kid sister about it, okay? She borrowed my car today and only just now does she get back with it. I told her all last night, Gabriella, *mija,* don't be screwing around with my wheels, okay? I'll get Bud after you!" She waved at Helen with a big smile and winked.

"So, Frieda, you bake this yourself?" she

27

marveled. "Mmm, girlfriend, you gonna make me forget to diet!"

Helen smiled at the dumb Mexican act Carmen put on. Everyone in the room knew she had proven herself to be an excellent secretary, responsive to the patients and conscientious about the complicated paperwork involved in a nonprofit organization.

"Well, I just got a call on my car phone from Janet Wilson. There's a big traffic jam on the Bay Bridge. Seems someone tried to make a new passing lane out over the water — skidded around and made a big ugly mess."

"What about Bob O'Neill? Where's he?" Jill asked.

"He left a message. His mom is back in the hospital, over in Daly City," Carmen said through a mouthful of bread and cheese.

"Damn. Well, I'd hate to call this off —" Dave broke off as the doorbell sounded again, and moments later Jill was following Melinda Wright into the room.

Helen knew that Dave had hired an accountant to examine the clinic's finances — Jill had muttered some dark things about the clinic's financial future — but she was surprised to see the woman here at the meeting. As far as Helen knew, the executive board had been called together to discuss Helen's findings after two weeks of working with the pro-life group in hopes of pinning down who was defacing the building and starting fires in the night. Why was an accountant here?

Carmen sniffed, set down her plate and crossed her legs tightly, refusing to acknowledge the woman's presence. What the hell was this all about? Helen wondered when Melinda nodded a greeting to everyone but Carmen. They must have clashed over paperwork, or something, Helen decided.

"Sit down, everyone, make yourselves at home." Jill padded around the room, playing hostess while Frieda disappeared in the depths of the house murmuring something about finishing a project in her studio.

"Looks like everyone's here who's gonna get here," Dave intoned. "I'll have to check up on Bob later tonight — that's the third time his mother's been in the hospital. Hope it isn't another stroke."

Melinda Wright sat primly on the edge of the sofa, her neat sensible shoes flat on the floor, her knees pressed together. She grimly refused Jill's offer of food or drink, even looked offended at the idea of edibles being offered at a meeting. She started when Carmen snapped her gum loudly and glanced in her direction over wire-rimmed glasses.

"Definitely got a stick up her butt," Jill whispered as she once again took her place on the cushions by the fire while Helen settled herself back into the overstuffed chair.

"Well, like I said, this is turning into a very informal meeting," Dave started. "Oh, by the way, Melinda, I don't think you've met Helen Black? She's the private investigator I was telling you about. The one that Jill — Dr. Mason here — recommended to us."

Helen smiled and shook hands, fighting off revulsion at the damp palm Melinda offered to her. "Hi."

Melinda neither smiled nor spoke, but went right back to her perch on the sofa and stacked file folders carefully in her lap. "Perhaps we could get started, Mr. Linville?"

"Yes, well, sure." He got up and stood before the fireplace, leaning against the mantel in a way that set off his chiseled profile. "I think, though, we should wait for Dolores, don't you?"

Melinda sighed. "I suppose we have no choice." She glanced down at her wristwatch, grimaced and folded her hands in her lap.

"So!" Dave grinned at everyone and ran a hand over his chin, struggling for a safe topic while they waited. "Oh, I meant to ask you, Jill — how's that new desk of yours?"

"Fine, Dave. Thanks again. That was nice of you to let me use it."

"Well, it's just been sitting around Grandma's old den for ages. It looked like it would fit, and it has locks and everything."

"Looks like they finally got the windows replaced, too."

"All of them? Really?"

"Yeah, the guys finished yesterday. When you comin' in, girlfriend, tomorrow?" Carmen asked. "Yeah, you'll see. Looks good."

"Well, that's a relief. It was getting really cold in that office."

Helen let her mind drift as Carmen, Jill and Dave went through office small talk. It had been the damaged desk and broken windows that inspired Jill's request for her services, she recalled. Helen had been surprised to hear the usually calm and mildly amused doctor sound so frantic and upset.

"The police seem to think it was some kind of, you know, what is it, Molotov cocktail or something,"

Jill had babbled. "I mean, I'm only at the clinic two days a week, but I keep everything in that desk, you know? And just think of what could have happened if anyone had been sitting there! Listen, Helen, all this shit — the fires, the paint, the protests — it's got to be stopped, somehow. I — well, I know you're probably really busy right now . . ."

"You mean, you'd like me to do a little detective work out there?" Helen had to admit she'd enjoyed drawing it out, making Jill break down and actually ask for her help. Of course, Frieda had put her up to it. Was Jill that pussy-whipped already?

"Well, maybe I could come out and take a look around for you. I'll have to check my calendar," Helen said, flipping through pristine pages of her daybook as she spoke. There'd been no activity in her expensive office for nearly a month, but she'd be damned if she leaped to take this job from the Magnificent Mason.

"I'd really appreciate it, Helen. We all would. I, well, I hate to say it, but after this last one, the fire in the office and the broken windows, we're all pretty scared."

It had taken only two days for the committee, led by Dave Linville, to agree to sign Helen's contract. Now, two weeks later, her report was —

Again the door opened, again a rush of cold damp air, this time scented with stale nicotine and bourbon. "Sorry I'm so late. People forget how to drive when it rains."

Helen suppressed a smile at the cringe warping Melinda Wright's prim features. With any luck Dolores would plop herself down right next to the accountant.

31

But even Dolores had a strong sense of survival. She went for the food right away, marveling at Jill's lovely, just *lovely* home, and settled into a chair close to Dave.

Actually, Helen observed, she was doing a pretty good job of hiding the fact that she'd knocked off a few at the bar down the road before attending the meeting. Except for a very slight flush in her cheeks that could have been from the fire, Dolores was all business.

Dave went through his litany of absent members once again for Dolores, but he kept it short when he noticed Melinda squirming and fiddling with her watch. "Okay, let's get started, people."

A few moments of minor details followed, involving things like the janitorial service then, "Okay, Helen. What have you got for us?"

Chapter Four

Half an hour later, Helen stood alone in the middle of Jill Mason's living room, her back to the fire, facing a handful of surprised faces. She'd expected them to be perturbed at the substance of her report, but this astonishment disconcerted her. Did they really think it would be that simple to investigate?

"Are you sure, Helen?" Dave asked. His worried face looked older in the firelight, and he rubbed his palms together with a dry rasping sound. "Not a single one of them?"

Helen sighed. Suddenly she felt very tired. Of course, everyone involved with the clinic was tired too — tired of being afraid, of dealing with the ugliness of it all, of the press and the crowds getting in the way of taking care of sick people. "Well, after two weeks of being with these people, day in and day out, my opinion is that none of the demonstrators have participated in the vandalism," she repeated.

"And just what do you base that on?" Dave asked, leaning back with a sigh of resignation.

"Up to this point, Dave, I've been sitting in on their meetings, talking to many of them personally, spending a great deal of time with them. You have to remember, it's going to take a while for an outsider like me to win their trust. If Dr. Logan and his followers are terrorizing the clinic with paint and fire and broken glass, they're going to be very careful about announcing that fact."

"Well, that's a whole lot of good!" Dolores blurted out. "What does that mean, that you have to be there for two years before you get anywhere?"

Carmen rolled her eyes and studied her nails in the glow of the fire. Melinda hunched herself more tightly over the files and set her lips in grim disapproval. Jill sat motionless on the cushions, staring at the floor.

Dave reached out an arm to pat Dolores's hand. "Now I'm sure Helen doesn't expect to be here for two years, Dolores. Why don't we give her a chance to tell us what she *is* going to do?"

Okay, Helen thought, here it comes. "There will be a strategy meeting at the church on Wednesday," she started, speaking very deliberately. "I'll be there with everyone else. While at the meeting I plan to raise the idea of stepping up the pressure a bit. Now," she went on, pacing the floor as their eyes fixed on her like a moving target, "I'm not going to be specific about this. I'm just going to suggest that maybe prayers aren't enough. Maybe the Lord wants us to take more drastic action."

"And that proves — what?" Carmen asked.

"Well, the idea is for the discussion to turn to the vandalism. If I'm able to get it going in that direction, I'll get a chance to see what the reactions are. Gauge the feelings there, get a sense of who it is I should question more closely. Then —"

Helen stopped when Jill threw a stray sliver of wood into the blaze behind her with a disgusted grunt. "Look, Helen, I'm sure you know your job, but honestly — where is all of this getting us?"

Helen stood and folded her arms across her chest. All the dislike for Jill she'd been battling for months reared up and she felt fury building inside. "What do you mean, Jill?" she said quietly.

"I'm sorry. I didn't mean to bark like that. It's just — well, we've all been sitting ducks for so long, not knowing where the next attack will come from! Jesus," she said, running both hands vigorously through her hair, "I don't know about the rest of you, but I feel like I have a bull's-eye painted on my back every damn time I walk up those steps into the clinic."

Helen looked down at her feet and waited a few moments for her angry reaction to subside. When she responded it was with as much calm and patience as she could muster. "Jill, don't think for a moment that I doubt the seriousness of what all of you face. All of you." She looked around the room to ensure

35

that everyone in the room knew she was addressing the entire group. "But I don't dare just march into that church on Wednesday, or confront them tomorrow, with empty accusations and threats. I have to learn about these people, find out what makes them tick, where they go and what they do. I have to learn their lives and beliefs before I can start focusing on who may or may not be involved. And the only way to do that is to be a part of it." She took a step closer to Jill and talked directly to the doctor, the heat from the fire flushing her cheeks and pulling beads of sweat through her scalp. "Get to know them on their terms first."

"So what comes after that?" Dolores wheezed from the other side of the room. She'd been fiddling a cigarette back and forth, around and around between her fingers, for the whole of Helen's recitation. "You'll maybe get around to finding something out when one of us gets shot? Huh?"

"Now, Dolores, come on. I really don't think —"

She cut Dave off with a wave of her hand and a cough. "Oh, come one, Dave! Quit playing macho man for once and face reality! We take a chance every damn time we go to work at the Linville."

"I don't think spray paint is the same thing as a bullet —"

"Bet that's just what those two women in Boston said that New Year's Eve. Remember? The ones that got killed by that right-wing freak?"

Dave sighed again and rubbed his eyes. Helen ducked her head to suppress a smile. Irritating as Dolores could be, she seemed to have a habit of hitting the nail rather bluntly on the head. In fact, that's probably why she *was* so irritating. Judging by the patiently exasperated look on Dave's face, he was feeling almost saintlike in his long-suffering willingness to deal with a pack of hysterical women. Any minute now he'd start making subtle hints about womanly vapors, or whatever the politically correct equivalent was these days. Meaning, of course, PMS.

"She's right, you know? I'm afraid to let my kid sister come by and drop off my car now, with all those damn people out there, and not knowing what Gabriella is going to see. *Mi madre,* she's not so crazy I'm working there, okay?" Carmen spoke sullenly, her full red lips pouting the words, but Helen saw the fear glittering in her eyes. "We don't know where it's coming from, so we don't know what to do."

"No one is denying we have a serious situation on our hands. All I'm saying is that we have to give Helen a chance to do her job, people."

Helen looked around the room again. Perhaps an informal meeting hadn't been such a good idea. Who had suggested it? Jill? Dave? However it had come about, the supposedly relaxed surroundings had done nothing to banish the fear. In fact, the more official setting of a conference room or an office might have given a calming effect of ceremony and formal proceedings. With everyone gathered around a fire as if sharing a cozy social evening with good friends, the tensions of dealing with potentially life-threatening situations on a daily basis broke through the slim veneer the clinic staff managed to maintain during working hours. At the Linville, these people had sick patients to care for, papers to fill out, records to maintain. They could channel their private fears into practical activity. Here, with all guards encouraged to dissipate, things were bound to get out of hand. Or, as Helen's late grandmother in Vicksburg would have said, emotion was so thick in there you could cut it with a butter knife.

"I'm not sure how much longer this can go on," Jill said. "I'm sorry, Helen, it's really not your fault." Helen nodded, then waited for her to continue. "It's just that — well, if it were just the demonstrators, it wouldn't be so bad. I mean, I agree with Helen. Most of them seem like basically decent people, doing something they believe in. At least, the ones I've seen here. But the fires, that red paint, the morning they left body parts — I mean, those doll parts — lying around! It's like it's all building up to something, some awful thing that's going to get someone hurt or even killed."

"What about the cops?" Dolores asked as she struggled up off the deep cushions of the sofa, jostling Melinda with a pointy elbow. "Can't they do anything?"

"The police have officers driving by and checking the place every night, you've put in the alarm system they suggested, and Bud is there every day now." Helen shrugged. "I'm sure they're doing a lot of questioning themselves. But they have to catch someone, and so far that hasn't happened. And," she said, heading back for her chair by the fire, "I guess no one is talking to them, any more than they will to me."

Jill snorted. "Police? That's a laugh! I wouldn't be surprised if they were in on it!"

"Why the hell do you say that?" Dolores said as she placed the well-handled cigarette between her lips and walked toward the sliding glass door facing the view of the bay.

"Oh, come on, Dolores! The only excitement Lafayette cops get is when someone runs the red light on First Street to get to the bridge so they won't be late for work!" Jill shook her head in disgust. "I'll bet you they're enjoying this. Especially since the clinic does Satan's work."

"Jesus, Jill," Dolores chuckled. She slid the door back with a quiet thud and rain blew into the room. "You've had a bug up your ass since the Summer of Love," and she walked out to the patio, ignoring the rain as she lit the cigarette.

"Summer of Love? You mean I missed it? No one ever tells me these things!"

Helen didn't know if Carmen was faking ignorance or not, but it served to shatter the tension in the room. As everyone laughed, Dave looked visibly relieved. "Well," he said heartily, "I move that we keep Helen on the job at least until the end of the month, if not longer. Actually, I guess that's only until the end of the week, isn't it? I almost forgot, Halloween is Saturday."

A moment of silence followed, then nods and murmurs of agreement circled the room. Dolores came back inside to give her assent along with the others.

Helen debated for the space of a minute whether to go or stay, since her part in the meeting was over. A glance outside at the steady rain, which was sure to be accompanied by intense cold winds, decided her in favor of the overstuffed chair and a plate of bread and cheese. She didn't think anyone would care.

Helen managed with success to distract herself until she heard Melinda Wright's high-pitched voice whine sharply into the warmth. "Regardless, Mr. Linville, I feel it's absolutely necessary to make my requests officially."

"Melinda, as I told you before, this is just a sort of bull session tonight, away from the stress of the office, to talk about a few issues. Surely we can all work this out together?"

Helen looked up in time to see Melinda's lips purse in distaste. "Well, since you insist, Mr. Linville. I find it absolutely impossible to go on with my audit."

Clearly everyone was bored and ready to go home. Helen swore she could hear a collective sigh.

"I've made several requests for paperwork and essential forms from — from various parties in the room, and I've had nothing but resistance all the way." The accountant kept her eyes on her stack of manila folders, plaiting her fingers together. "Unless I receive full cooperation from the staff, I won't be able to continue and have a report ready for the Board of Directors at the end of the year."

"What are you talking about? I gave you everything you asked for. I'd even hand over my box of Kleenex, if I thought it would help!" Dolores subsided when no one laughed at her joke, slumping sullenly on the sofa next to Melinda.

Melinda stood up. "I really have nothing further to say. Without cooperation, I can't make a recommendation to the Board regarding the clinic's future. When I come in tomorrow, I expect everyone to supply me with the information I need." She snapped shut her dark leather briefcase. "If there's nothing else, I have a few more things to do at the clinic before I go home."

"Recommendation? What recommendation?" Jill asked Dave as soon as she returned from seeing Melinda out the front door.

"I didn't think I needed to go into this tonight. Not yet. Oh, hell, you had to hear about it anyway."

"What?" Even Carmen sat up, alert, worried.

"It looks like there might not be any Linville Clinic after next year."

Dave stood quietly, hands stuffed into pockets, while the others muttered in disbelief.

"But the Linville Trust! I mean, it's a nonprofit organization. Doesn't the Trust keep the clinic going?"

"It really isn't that simple, Jill. They do, but the Trust is operated by a committee, just like this one. I'm on that committee, like I'm on this one and several others, but I'm only one voice. Of course, I'll do all I can to keep things going, but . . ."

"But?"

"The Trust is worded so that it funds a whole bunch of charitable organizations. The clinic is only one of them. Each five years, ever since my grandmother died, the board reviews the operations of these charities, and makes a decision about whether or not to fund them."

"In other words, we have to pass a midterm."

"Basically, yes, Carmen." Dave looked around the room, his expression dripping apologies. "That's why I brought Melinda in. She'd been recommended to me by quite a few people as a thorough worker."

"So I'm just supposed to let her go through all my files, my private files, to paw around through my

41

patients' lives? Is that it?" Jill glared at Dave from her station by the fireplace. She gathered her knees up to her chin and sat there, barely containing her fury. "It'll be a cold day in hell before that fucked-up establishment bitch comes near my files. "

"Jill, I know you don't mean that." Dave switched to kindly uncle again, his voice edged with anger. "She doesn't want your private files, she wants to see requisitions for drugs, for supplies, things like that. Nothing else. All right?" He took Jill's silence to mean assent, then looked at the others. "And that goes for all of us. The future of the Linville Memorial Clinic may very well depend on what she has to tell the board."

Solemn words, Helen thought, watching the others slowly file out of the house. At some point Frieda reappeared, her fingers stained with paint and an old tunic tossed over her clothes. Helen left after making a couple of feeble attempts to help in the kitchen. It only took one real refusal to encourage her to go — Jill and Frieda clearly wanted time to themselves.

The rain had stopped when she got into her car. It had been a very strange evening. There was something unreal about it all. A performance. But for who? And who had staged it, after all?

Never mind, Helen told herself. Better get home and feed the cat. Boobella was sure to meet her at the door, crying and scratching, complaining about the sad, lonely life she led as a pampered feline queen. With a start, Helen jumped away from the car seat. What the hell — it was that damned cell phone again. She'd have to remember to bring it inside with her from now on instead of tempting any casual thief by displaying it in full view on the front seat of her car.

Briefly, as Helen steered her car westward toward Berkeley, she glanced out at the scattered lights of Lafayette, wondering which house belonged to Allison Young.

Chapter Five

Helen got up and moved away from the fence post where she'd been waiting. Weren't those Logans ever going to show up with that coffee? Damn, it was cold. And she'd forgotten her gloves again. She couldn't believe she hadn't already gotten the flu by now. Allison probably wouldn't be around today. Generally she showed up on Mondays and Wednesdays.

Great, Helen lectured herself. The woman doesn't even know you exist, and already you're thinking about the next time you're going to see her. She flashed back to the man who'd been whispering Allison's name the day before and felt a quiver of anxiety. Something very wrong there.

Another couple equipped with Bibles walked over the gravel, smiling at Helen. She nodded back. They were joined by an elderly woman with a sweet smile and a poster of an aborted fetus in her gloved hands.

"Oh, hi, Helen! You got here early today!"

How the hell did Donna contrive to look so bright and alert every morning? Helen could have slapped her for that perky little voice, but she smiled at Donna instead, stretching almost frozen lips over gritted teeth. "Thought I'd beat the freeway traffic. How's that runny nose this morning?"

"Oh, as soon as I woke up, the Lord had taken my cold away! I feel just great! Ready to do His work."

"Good, good." Helen asked, "Where is everyone else? I thought Dr. Logan would be here by now." With coffee.

"Oh, I'm sure they're on the way." Together they looked at the front of the clinic. The black smudges from smoke were the same ones that stained the wall yesterday, and the red paint had faded beneath the rain and scrubbing applied the day before. "Looks like no one was here last night, doesn't it?"

Helen walked closer. "You're right. Nothing new." Helen was curious. So far there had been no pattern to the activities of the vandals. The incidents occurred at least twice a week, sometimes on successive nights, sometimes in intervals of two to three days. There had always been two separate means used, sometimes three — paint, fire, broken windows. Only on the first occasion had they left the

45

doll parts dipped in red paint. It was as if whoever was behind this had had the wisdom to restrain their eagerness, not to push their luck. Of course, it could be just one person, but Helen was certain that there had to be teamwork involved to complete the destruction successfully. Someone to keep watch, several people to carry out the work of defacement quickly and efficiently. "I'm sorry, Donna, what did you say?"

But Donna didn't answer. She was walking toward the ancient Chevy station wagon pulling up on the gravel of the parking lot. Dr. and Mrs. Logan emerged from the creaking doors, and Mrs. Logan, beaming at the two women already at the clinic, trotted in her galoshes to the back of the car. Moments later an array of doughnuts and Styrofoam cups and coffee cake were spread across the tailgate.

Helen gratefully accepted a cup of coffee, black, and selected a doughnut covered with white frosting and chocolate sprinkles. She was too hungry and cold to think about freshness or nutrition, and she gratefully bit into the greasy dough.

"This is wonderful, Mrs. Logan. Thank you."

"Oh, you're welcome, dear! There, do you think that will be enough?"

"It's the early bird that gets the worm — or the doughnut!" They chuckled a bit too heartily at Dr. Logan's innocent joke, and Helen reached for the thermos and a refill on the coffee. "Still, you can never be too early to do God's work, can you, Helen?"

"No sir, never," she agreed. Uncomfortably she realized that this was the first time Dr. Logan had addressed her by her first name. Was it a sign of acceptance, or a warning signal she should heed?

"Tell me again, Helen, what church are you with?"

"Well, sir, it's just a small congregation. Actually, we started it ourselves. A bunch of us were just not satisfied with the lack of Scripture study at our church, so we just began meeting in different houses," Helen began, the well-rehearsed story spilling easily out of her.

"Just like the early Christians." Dr. Logan nodded in approval.

"That's what we were hoping, sir! That if we could follow the Lord like they did, we would get closer to Him and find out His plan for us."

Dr. Logan sipped his coffee, his bird-like beak of a nose bobbing over the steam rising from the cup. "So many of our brothers and sisters in Christ have drifted away from the holy word of God. They don't study their Bible or make the scriptures part of their daily lives. It's good to know that there are true Bible Christians in Berkeley these days."

Another car crunched over the gravel, and Bud Griffin's enormous red four-wheel drive ground to a halt across the parking area from the Logans' humbler vehicle.

"Morning, sir! Cup of hot coffee?"

Bud grinned and waved. "Maybe in a minute, Reverend. Gotta make my rounds first. Thanks anyway," and the bulky figure in blue trudged off around the side of the building. He always started by inspecting the back, then working his way around to the front.

"You know, he seems like such a nice guy," Donna said to Helen. "I don't know why a man as sweet as that would want to do this kind of work."

"Now, Donna, we're not here to judge anyone," Mrs. Logan chirped. She stood by her husband, patting his hands in her own to keep them warm. "If he *is* a good man, and I'm sure you're right, then the Lord will show him the light in His own good time."

"Seems to me like the clinic people would want a security guard here all the time," Donna went on. "What with all those nasty words painted on at night and all."

"Guard duty costs money. See up there? That black box by the door? And there's another one over at the end of the building." They followed Dr. Logan's gesture and looked at the alarm signal boxes poking out from under the eaves of the roof. "That's what those are for. They're probably rigged up to the police station, to give an alarm when someone tries to break in."

"Well, they sure aren't working too well!" Donna laughed. "Guess the Lord is sending a message to them, isn't He?"

Helen sipped coffee and watched the Logans exchange a glance. It was amazing to think of the signals a long-married couple could send each other with just a look. The Logans stiffened like statues for the space of a minute at the mention of the vandalism, then resumed their usual cheerful expressions.

Dr. Logan shook his head and smiled gently at Donna. "That's not for me to say, honey. All I know is we're here to pray for these people and help them to see the truth and mend their ways."

For a moment Helen felt ashamed that she'd suspected this sweet old man of anything so ridiculous and petty and mean as spray-painting obscenities on walls. A wave of memory swept over her, and suddenly she was back in Mississippi, running away from home after the beating her father gave her for being a perversion and a curse. The first person she'd gone to was their minister, who'd always exuded kindness and gentleness. And with his usual kind and gentle smile, he'd turned Helen away and left her to fend for herself, at seventeen, with nowhere to go and no one to turn to.

"I'm afraid I can't help you. No one can help you but God. Even He will turn against you if you persist in defying His command and living this unclean life."

Helen shook herself away from the memory, glad to find herself in California, in the winter, holding a cup of coffee in her hands and working on a case, as far away as possible from those days of pain and loneliness.

"Here, Mom." The young man carrying a box of doughnuts — more supplies for the demonstrators — bore a striking facial resemblance to Dr. Logan. The same beaked nose, tiny dark eyes and weak chin faced Helen with boredom. The likeness ended there, however. This younger version of the preacher wore his baseball cap backwards, his jeans low on his hips and an oversize T-shirt over his skinny frame.

"Hi, Cam!" Donna called out. "Are you here to pray with us today?"

The young man glanced up at her with a look that verged on a sneer, making no attempt to conceal his disgust. He shook his head without speaking as he plopped the box down on the tailgate, sloshing cups onto the gravel and smashing a couple of doughnuts in the process.

"It'd sure be nice to have you! And the other kids," Donna persisted. He rolled his eyes and turned his acne-ridden face away, as if ignoring the woman would make her go away.

"So can I borrow the car now, Dad?"

"Now, Cambridge, I already told you we'll need it today for delivering these leaflets over to the Sunnyside congregation. Unless you want to go over there yourself. I know Brother Johnson could use a hand with repainting the fellowship hall."

"Forget it. Later."

Mrs. Logan patted her son on the cheek, oblivious to the way he flinched at her touch. "Oh, thank you, son. Oh, and Cambridge, would you please remember to take that package over to Mrs. Bridges? I know she's been waiting for those clothes for the kids."

"Yeah, right, Mom." Cam Logan shuffled off from the car, rolling his eyes as he turned away. Donna and Helen caught themselves staring, then busied themselves with pulling picket signs and leaflets out of the back seat of the station wagon.

"He's a real cross to bear for his parents," Donna whispered as they bent over stacks of pamphlets. "They can't seem to do a thing with him. They need our prayers."

"Really? What's he done?"

"Well . . ." Donna looked over her shoulder. Dr. Logan and his wife were safely out of range, setting out the doughnuts Cam had brought. "I think he's into skateboards, and they say he has a tattoo. Honestly, I don't understand how these boys —"

"Will you look at that!"

Donna and Helen scrambled out of the car in time to see Bud running over the gravel, blue jacket flying in the morning wind, a few strands of hair waving wildly over his eyebrows. Helen wouldn't have believed that such a large man could move so quickly. As he came closer, Helen saw that his eyes bugged out in fear and his face was a broad circle of pallor above the blue uniform shirt. Sweating profusely, he panted and gasped as he stopped in front of the Logans.

"Out there — back of clinic — help —"

Helen made out the words before the others did. Without waiting to explain she left Bud standing there with Donna and the Logans and took off at a run in the direction Bud had just come from. "Get on the phone right away — there's a cell phone in my car — and get the police out here. Now, damnit!" In her urgency she forgot to restrain her words, and as she darted away she tossed her car keys back to Donna. With a last glance over her shoulder she saw Donna standing with the keys clutched in one small gloved hand, her mouth a pink O below huge surprised blue eyes. Mrs. Logan was huddled over Bud, who stood by the station wagon retching, his bulk heaving as he bent over.

Her feet flew over the gravel, kicking up small stones behind her, hoping she'd misunderstood the aging guard. Remembering his pale face and horrified eyes, though, she dreaded what she'd find behind the Linville.

The gravel parking lot ended at the side of the building, abruptly cut off by thick grass that still bloomed a deep green from the spurt of growth provided by the recent rain. Weeds bunched here and there, sprawling across the grass and tangling around Helen's legs. A chain-link fence, recently repaired

51

from where the nightly visitors had left their mark, slowed her down only for a second or two. She climbed it easily and hurried through more grass and weeds to the narrow frontage road that ran in back of the clinic grounds.

Built before the arrival of rapid transit to Lafayette, the frontage road barely squeezed two lanes out of one. Edged with mud that threatened to encroach on the battered asphalt every winter, the neglected road could be used as a shortcut to the freeway. That is, if one didn't mind potholes and cracked pavement that bloomed with stubborn plant growth. No one had ever bothered to suggest that lighting would be a good idea, since the road had been doomed to misuse for years. Still, if you were in a hurry to get through the increasingly congested traffic of downtown Lafayette, which was bursting at the seams with refugees from urban life in San Francisco, the frontage road, which never had a name as far as Helen knew, would bypass all the honking cars and careless pedestrians. Oddly enough, it had never become popular as a lover's lane — perhaps because it was just too dark and isolated for romance. The only thing it had in its favor was the nearness of a stream that curved around the outskirts of the city and had so far eluded developers because it wasn't in the way of anything they wanted. In their wisdom the city fathers had decided that the road was not worth its upkeep, so weeds and dirt and rocks threatened to spill over, creating yet another set of obstacles for the hapless motorist.

Helen picked her way as quickly as she could, knowing she might bump against one of these hidden rocks. She stopped to catch her breath after struggling through the unforgiving foliage. She panted out white frosty air into the cold morning. What had Bud seen, what had frightened him, what —

There it was. Sunlight in narrow shafts spiked through the clouds gathering overhead that signaled yet another storm. The beams glinted off the white Toyota sitting idle at the side of the road.

By now the police would be on their way. Helen, determined to see what she could before the place was sealed off, crept slowly and carefully through the grass until she reached the road. Careful to stay on the asphalt and watch where she walked, she cautiously approached the car. Except for the vehicle, the road was completely empty.

Helen recognized the shoes on the corpse splayed across the front seat of the car. They were the ones Melinda had worn last night.

Chapter Six

Hell. Isn't this rain ever going to fucking stop?

Behind Helen, over on a relatively smooth patch of grass, Donna languished in the arms of a handsome young police officer. She'd come rushing around the building, her high-heeled boots stubbing in a staccato along the cracked asphalt of the frontage road, paying no attention to Helen's demands that she stay away and wait for the police. The moment she'd seen the body of Melinda Wright in the car Donna had slumped over in shock on the wet grass. That was how the police had found the two of them, squatting in the wet grass at the side of the road.

Better that than the police seeing Helen peering into the car, absorbing as much detail as her mind would allow before she was ushered away. Now yellow tape marked with bold black letters announcing a warning to stay away from the crime scene flapped in the breeze that had gotten colder and stiffer since Helen had viewed the body.

She'd already been questioned briefly, and she was now waiting for an officer to allow her to leave the scene. Bud Griffin, as the first to find Melinda, had had the honors of being grilled by the police about who Melinda was, what she was doing there and the details of his discovery. While biding her time and pacing to keep warm, Helen went back over the mental notes she'd taken of the scene.

Both front doors of Melinda Wright's Toyota were open to the elements, and from the side of the road Helen saw that the rain had washed into the car. Water was still dripping from the edge of the door, and the carpet and seats were soaked with rain and blood. It was an ugly death — Helen couldn't be sure how many shots had been fired, but the gun must have been no more than a yard away from Melinda's head. Her feet stuck out of the driver's side, one beige leather pump nearly falling off the stiffening body, and she was lying with her head in the direction of the passenger door. In fact, her hand was stretched out toward the open door, as if in her last moments she'd been trying to get out of the car away from the driver's side. Her conservative beige suit was much less rumpled than it would have been if Melinda had struggled with her killer. It was soaked through from the rain but relatively intact. And there was no overcoat in sight. Helen couldn't imagine someone so meticulous and fastidious forgetting a coat, or venturing into inclement weather without one. Strange.

With the wind and the rain the night before, Helen doubted there would be much evidence to glean from the Toyota. The keys were still in the ignition, and it appeared that the car had been left running, gears placed in a parking position, until the gasoline was used up. Helen had walked to the front of the car and seen the headlights flicker, then fade as the battery gave out.

Rain was already playing havoc with everything, Helen realized, as huge cold drops pelted her head and face. She zipped up her coat and pulled the hood up snugly over her hair, continuing all the while to examine the car without touching anything. When the police arrived, they'd do their best to cover the place and photograph everything before it washed away in the storm, but they'd have to move fast.

There was no reason why the killer should have left any evidence in the car, anyway. He or she could have opened the door on the driver's side — threatened Melinda, who attempted to get out through the passenger door — then fired the shot or series of shots that ended her life. Or perhaps Melinda herself opened the driver's door. The killer might have been someone she knew.

Then there was the empty can of spray paint. As Helen had walked away from the car, she'd felt her foot nudge something that moved. Crouching down she peered under the Toyota, grubbed up a stick from the side of the road, and saw the metal rim of the can as it rolled in response to her gentle push. A swath of red on the label, streaked with mud, indicated the paint's color, and Helen was certain the paint would turn out to match the red used on the graffiti still visible on the clinic's walls.

The most obvious thing at the scene was the absence of the gun. Helen wondered if there was some way to find out ballistics information. Maybe Manny, her former partner who still worked for the Berkeley police, could do some checking later on for her. Of course the stream, rushing noisily through the grassy ravine on the north side of the road, was the obvious place to look.

Obvious. Helen chewed on the word while all around her the police did their job, questioning and photographing and crawling back and forth over the Toyota, blithely examining Melinda as if her body were a part of the car's upholstery. That was the problem. Somehow the whole thing felt too obvious. The dramatic placement of the body in the middle of the road. The empty can of paint. A handy little creek nearby that would keep the police occupied for quite a while, searching its muddy waters for information. Even the dark and stormy night, and the nearness of Halloween. It felt like the board game Helen had played as a kid, where Mr. Plum murders Mrs. Peacock with the rope in the conservatory. The scene was all bits and pieces that seemed significant by themselves but made no sense when all put together.

She looked up again as a camera flashed nearby. A photographer was busily recording the morass of footprints in the mud at the side of the road, next to the car. From what Helen had seen, it was doubtful that any sense would be made of those imprints. The mud had been so slippery from the rain that no clear outlines were visible. As she watched the photographer at work, Helen was reminded of Jill's comment about the Lafayette police the evening before. Was she accurate in her assessment? Granted, murder probably wasn't a common occurrence in this town, but would these guys do everything they should?

Helen smiled to herself wryly at her own presumption. She'd turned in her badge several years ago — time to back off. Just round up the usual suspects, and then —

Then it hit her. The people gathered at Jill's house last night may have been the last people to see Melinda alive, except for the killer. What time had that broken up? Around nine, Helen thought. So far, because Bud had borne the brunt of the questioning, Helen's own acquaintance with Melinda Wright and the Linville Clinic hadn't been brought up. Of course before she left she'd look for the lieutenant and tell him about her investigation. Melinda had said she was going back to the clinic to finish some work — she must have been entrusted with the security codes for the alarm system. Who else would be at the clinic at night? Had she surprised the vandals in the act? Then why not just call the police from inside the clinic, in safety? Why go out to her car — unless the clinic itself was not safe?

"Just like back East," a voice mumbled close by. Helen swiveled around to see who had spoken. Donna looked up, her lower lip trembling and her eyes brimming with unshed tears, at the young officer who supported her in his strong embrace.

"Like those other women at those clinics," he went on. "Starts with vandalism, next thing you know somebody gets hurt."

"Rehnquist!"

"Yes, sir!" The officer patted Donna's arm and gently disengaged himself from her clutches. "You'll be fine, miss," he murmured as he went back toward the car and his superiors.

Donna looked over to Helen and approached her with unsteady steps. "Oh, Helen, I've been praying and praying for that woman's soul! Who could do such a thing?"

"I don't know, Donna. I'm sure the police will find the killer," Helen said soothingly as her mind raced over what she'd seen.

"Maybe it's a sign — maybe she was coming here to get an abortion!" Donna whispered.

Helen started to answer, then stopped herself. Good point. Where *had* Melinda been going? The Toyota was pointed in the direction of the freeway, but if Melinda was originally driving east, she could also have been heading back into town. Helen was certain the frontage road split off just past the BART station in two directions. One would take Melinda to the freeway toward San Francisco — the other led into the outskirts of Lafayette, where a few crumbling apartment buildings, the closest thing Lafayette had to a ghetto, sagged on winding narrow streets. Where did Melinda live, anyway? And who would know more about her?

Even though Helen didn't think it likely that the vandals had killed Melinda, she itched to find out more about the dead woman. Surely someone, Dave or Jill or Dolores, would know more.

"All right, all right, everyone just back off, now! Let's give these folks a chance to do their work!" Near the center of the road, pressed up as close to the yellow tape as the police would allow, the curious citizenry of Lafayette fought for a look at the body. Helen spotted one or two familiar faces in the crowd close to where she stood, off to the side in the grass. For the most part the ghoulish cluster of onlookers knotted on the pavement, avoiding the cold damp grass. There was the couple that had arrived early for the demonstration, still clutching their Bibles for dear life. And that man over there was a frequent visitor to the Linville.

"Are you girls all right?" Mrs. Logan waded across the grass, Dr. Logan faltering behind her. "We were so worried, Helen, when you ran off like that!"

"Oh, Mrs. Logan!" Donna found a new source of comfort in the elderly woman's soft bosom, and Dr. Logan stood behind them, lips pursed and head bowed thoughtfully.

"Some of the brothers and sisters are gathering right now in a prayer circle for this poor young woman," he intoned. "I thought you and Donna might like to join us."

Donna left without a backward glance, and soon the minister and his wife were surrounded by a faithful band of disciples. They were too engrossed in their goal to notice that Helen stayed behind, watching the crowd. Within five minutes the small group of faithful had gathered in a circle, holding hands, behind the crowd squeezed up against the barrier. People pushed and shoved past them, and Helen saw that Dr. Logan was nearly knocked over a couple of times.

Quit looking for her, Helen ordered herself. No way Allison Young was going to be in this crowd. She wasn't the type. Besides, this wasn't her day to volunteer at the clinic.

"Hey, look out, sonofabitch!" There was no mistaking that shrill voice. Carmen Espinoza stood just beyond the prayer circle, craning her neck and cursing at the teenagers pushing their way closer to the front of the crowd. She hadn't spotted Helen yet. At Carmen's side was a thin young girl, no more than fourteen or fifteen, Helen guessed. Her lank brown hair was stuffed under a baseball cap, and a sweatshirt three sizes too big hung over the faded jeans that sported fashionably wide holes at the knees. A few wisps of hair escaped from the cap and fluttered on the breeze that smelled like rain.

"You know Mama is gonna kill you, dummy! What are you doing here?" Carmen hissed at the girl.

Helen couldn't hear the response, but the girl's expression was a mixture of frustration and fear. Carmen and the girl exchanged a few more words, then the girl ran away through the grass and around the side of the clinic.

"Gabi! *Ven aqui, pronto!* " Carmen shouted after her sister, threw up her hands in exasperation and turned back to stare at Melinda's car. She stayed for another couple of minutes, then slowly turned around and went in the same direction as her sister.

The crowd broke up with cries of irritation as the downpour started in earnest. People scattered all over the road, hurrying out through the narrow shoulder between the clinic's fence and the side of the road. The creek, already roiling furiously from the previous storms, sloshed up against the mud and splattered the shoes of the detectives crouched close to the ground by the Toyota.

Helen didn't think she ought to stay any longer. She didn't need to be noticed. Trailing along after Dr. Logan and the faithful, she and the little band of protesters left just as the ambulance arrived. Without any need for sirens or speed, the ambulance humped along the uneven pavement, lurching its way to its passenger. Helen turned away quickly, not wanting to see this final cloak of anonymity enforced on Melinda. Did she have family here? Who would care that she'd died, or grieve for the loss?

Dr. Logan gathered the bedraggled group under the dripping eaves at the side of the clinic. "I think we'd just better go on home, everybody," he shouted over the wind howling around the building. "We should stay out of the way of the police, and let's just go on home now and pray to our heavenly father for the soul of this woman."

Murmured amens showed agreement, and the little cluster broke up and ran for cars and warmth and safety. Helen lingered, walking toward her car and waiting there, fumbling with her keys until the last car had pulled away. Then she hurried through the downpour to the clinic's entrance.

"I'm sorry, ma'am, I'm not allowed to let anyone in without a pass." The young security guard who had replaced Bud stood at the door with military correctness. "I have very strict orders."

Helen sighed, bit off a retort, then asked, "Could you please find Dolores Wayne? She'll vouch for me. That's Dolores Wayne, Administrative Director."

A minute later Dolores hurried her inside. "Yes, yes, it's fine. Come on in, Helen. You must be dead from cold. Wait a minute —" She stopped outside her office. "Did the saints see you come in?"

"The — oh, no. They've all gone. I was just hoping I could use a phone in here."

"Why not! Look, I'm going to have to go with Dave to talk to those cops for a minute, so you can use my office. Whoops!" In hurrying out Dolores ran smack into Jill. "What are you doing here today?"

"Dr. Magnuson asked me to cover for him this morning. What's going on? Did something else happen last night?"

Dolores led her off down the hall, chattering excitedly about the murder. Helen closed the door and dialed a number she knew by heart. Unfortunately Manny Hernandes had his pager switched on, which could mean any number of things. Helen frowned, pressed in her cell phone number and decided to go back home and see what she could find out about Melinda Wright. There was no telling — this murder might have some connection with the vandalism she was investigating, after all.

As Helen left Dolores Wayne's office, she saw two police officers, uniformed, talking to someone at the end of the corridor. One of the officers moved aside, and Jill's face, tense and pale, looked out at her.

After a further exchange, the officers nodded to each other. Jill looked up at them, angry, then resigned. She slipped out of her lab coat and the trio proceeded down the hall, pushing their way through the throng of patients waiting for attention. One or two of them reached out to Jill, confused at the sight of their doctor going away.

"My God," Dolores whispered. Helen jumped. She hadn't heard her come up. Dolores took no notice of her surprise. "Are they arresting Jill?" she asked eagerly. "What's going on?"

Helen turned around. Dolores was flushed enough to have started drinking already — did she have liquor for breakfast? — and Helen smelled the odor of a recent cigarette as the woman breathed heavily over her shoulder. "I don't know," she said as she quickly pushed her way through the hall to Jill's side. The eyes of Dolores, and of a lot of other people, watched the little parade from the end of the corridor to the entrance.

"I'm sure it's nothing, Helen," Jill said, forcing a smile on her lips. "They just want me to answer a few questions about the meeting last night."

About the argument you and Melinda had, Helen thought. Did Dolores say something to them about it? Just outside the doorway, which was wide open to the elements, a stocky man in a black raincoat stood, flipping through a notepad and talking to another uniformed officer. Helen recognized that look, the way he seemed so unobtrusive and so insinuating at the same time — he must be the lieutenant in charge.

"Jill —"

She turned and said, "Don't worry, Helen. They still allow one phone call, don't they?"

Chapter Seven

"Helen, they had Jill in there for hours! I can't believe the police would do that if they didn't suspect her of something!"

Helen adjusted the telephone more comfortably between her shoulder and her ear. The wool pullover she'd dug up from the front closet was beautifully warm but its fuzzy surface scratched her cheek. Helen strained to open the bottle of scotch with one last twist before the cap yielded. With a grateful sigh she poured the golden liquid into her glass.

"Frieda, I'm not saying you don't have something

serious to deal with here. All I want is for you to realize that there's precious little you can do at the moment. Now, Jill's asleep, you said?"

A heavy sigh at the other end, then Frieda said, "I think so. We talked for a little bit, then she couldn't keep her eyes open anymore. I'm sort of worried, to be honest."

"She's probably just exhausted from all the tension."

Helen heard another heavy sigh. "Not only that, she insisted on going back to the clinic to help out. Since Carmen disappeared —"

"What do you mean?"

"She's gone. No one has seen her since the police were there. Took off, left her desk a mess, they didn't have anyone to answer the phones . . ."

Helen remembered Carmen arguing with a much younger woman near Melinda's car. "Interesting. No one can find her?"

"No, so Jill decided to stay and help out, pick up the slack. She just came home and fell into bed. Helen, I'm — I'm really scared. I mean, does she need to call a lawyer?"

Helen had to smile. After all those years, after listening to Frieda complain about everything connected with law enforcement and detective work, who did she turn to when she needed help? Feeling slightly ashamed of her smug reaction, Helen did her best to reassure her ex-lover.

"I hope you're right. Listen, Helen, I'm sorry I bent your ear for so long. It was just — well, I knew you'd understand what was happening."

"That's okay. What else are ex-girlfriends for?" At that remark, Manny Hernandes shifted from his position on the sofa in Helen's living room and made a face at her, rolling his eyes. Helen saluted him with the bottle of scotch, raising her eyebrows and pointing at the bottle. Manny nodded at her unspoken offer and set another glass on the counter.

"I'll call you tomorrow, okay? Try not to worry too much, Frieda." Moments later Helen left her kitchen, walked through the narrow dining room and sat down next to her former partner, bringing the scotch with her. Manny took the second glass from her hand.

"Hey, don't drop that stuff! Don't want to waste it." He sipped at it, sighed with pleasure and turned his attention back to the television set.

Helen settled into the sofa and gulped the scotch down. Medicinal, she told herself, savoring the glow that washed over her tired bones. There was a rustle behind her in the dining room, then a black feline blur darted over Manny's legs and landed square on Helen's lap.

"Damn cat! Who invited you?" Boobella ignored the mock anger in Helen's voice and rubbed her broad face against the scratchy wool sweater. "I don't care what you say, you're not getting any scotch."

"Hey, you stupid kitty!" Manny absently scratched under the cat's chin. Boobella flopped over on her back and sprawled willingly for the human attention. "Long time no see."

"Don't you dare call her stupid," Helen muttered after another sip. "This cat has outlasted all my girlfriends."

"You okay, *amigo*? I mean, I know it hasn't been that long since she left . . ."

"Yeah, I'm fine. Don't worry about me." Helen

eased the cat down between herself and Manny, then grabbed the remote from the floor. "Looks like they're playing our song now."

The volume boomed up and the flaxen-haired anchor, the one with the nose job and the facial tucks, stared earnestly into the camera and spoke about Lafayette. Behind her on the screen a box was inset that showed a silhouette of a gun. "We go now live to Lafayette, in Contra Costa County. Bill?"

The screen switched to a jerky video camera's view of the outside the clinic. "Joyce, I'm standing here outside of the Linville Memorial Clinic, in the East Bay suburb of Lafayette. This morning, the peaceful bedroom town was horrified to wake up to something that you wouldn't expect to find in these peaceful, quiet streets — murder."

This somber announcement was followed by footage of past newscasts, showing the crowds of demonstrators and the damage to the building left by the vandals. Dramatically, Bill intoned a brief history of the disturbances at the Linville, interspersed with "man-on-the-street" comments from a handful of Lafayette residents.

Joyce's taut waxy features reappeared on the screen. "Bill, I understand that Dave Linville, heir to the Linville millions and head of the clinic's executive board gave a press conference today. Do we have any footage of that?"

"Yes, Joyce. The following was taped earlier this afternoon, after an emergency meeting of the Trustees of the Ida Linville Charitable Foundation."

Helen leaned forward on the sofa, nudging aside an irritated cat that protested with a whining mew. Where the hell were they? Looked like a hotel lobby — maybe that wedding cake building, the Duck Hunter Hotel, that graced one end of Mt. Diablo Boulevard. That seemed an appropriate venue for a conference held by such a respectable organization. Helen wondered briefly just how much money the Trust controlled — and how much influence Dave had with them.

An ashen-faced Dave Linville, dressed in a dark suit, strode up to a bank of microphones. Six men — no, six men and one woman — arranged themselves with folded hands and grave faces behind him as he spoke.

"The meeting this afternoon was called to initiate a review of the clinic's activities in light of the — uh, the recent developments," he said lamely. "Like all the other organizations that receive funding from the Trust, the clinic here in Lafayette comes up for review by the Trustees every five years to decide — to *discern* whether or not that funding is appropriate —"

"Are they gonna close the clinic down, Mr. Linville?" a reporter shouted from the back of the room.

Dave tried to ignore the clamor from the cameras and people, but question after question surged up to him from the crowd.

"Is the murder connected to the pro-life demonstrations?"

"Will the murder be the straw that breaks the back of the Linville?"

"Is Lafayette willing to allow the clinic to stay open after today?"

Finally, his face flushed with anger, Dave held up both hands until the noise subsided. The line of trustees behind him hadn't moved since the shouting began, but their faces were rigid with distaste for this display of crude vulgarity. As the room quieted down Dave gestured off-camera to his left. "I have up here with me," he said, "Dr. Howard Logan, minister of the United Pentecostal Church of Christ in God here in Lafayette. Dr. Logan?"

Helen and Manny glanced at each other. This was a surprise. Absently Helen reached down to scratch between Boobella's ears, and the cat loosened her tenacious grip on Helen's leg and melted into a contented purr.

Sure enough, the wizened little man, looking shriveled and exhausted in front of the merciless television cameras, squeezed his way past a troop of reporters. He cleared his throat several times. Beads of sweat trickled down over the beak nose and his voice, overworked today, no doubt, rasped into the microphones. Helen saw a flimsy sheet of paper trembling in his hands. Logan avoided looking up at the cameras, fixing his gaze on the paper that crackled beneath the microphones.

"Mr. Linville and I," he began, "have been talking today about the tragedy at the clinic. The elders of my congregation have decided unanimously to halt the public prayer sessions for tomorrow, as a memorial to this young woman so savagely attacked by a godless sinner. This in no way —" he looked up for emphasis — "in no way is a show of capitulation to the forces of evil at work in this town. We will not give up our fight for the rights of the unborn. However, we ask all our fellow worshippers to pray for those defenseless babies in the privacy of their own homes, and join us at the church tomorrow morning for a special meeting. At this meeting we will discuss future activities, and ask for the Lord's help and guidance in this difficult time." When he stopped to clear his throat, the shouting started up again.

"Why are you spray-painting the walls, Logan?"

"Did your elders condone the murder of Melinda Wright?"

"Is your church part of the militia terrorist underground?"

Dave gently pushed the quaking minister aside and spoke loudly and angrily into the microphones. "What Dr. Logan was about to say was that I will be in attendance at the church tomorrow morning. Together I believe the Linville Memorial Clinic and his congregation here in Lafayette can reach a peaceful and appropriate solution to our differences. Dr. Logan —" He looked up. "Quiet, please!"

Dave's protests were in vain. The noise overcame his words, and with a disgusted look on his face Dave led Dr. Logan away from the microphones, past the dour glances of the Trustees and out of the camera's eye.

Helen muted the sound when Joyce's face reappeared. "Shit, I don't think anyone is expecting that. The place will be crawling with reporters tomorrow."

"The church or the clinic?" Manny asked as he helped himself to more scotch.

"Both, I'm sure. Well, it probably won't be anything like the church meetings I used to go to as a kid."

The news was now focused on sports, and silently a football moved in slow motion across the screen of Helen's TV set. "What did you find out about

Melinda today?" Helen asked Manny as they stared at the instant replay.

"Great. I go to all the trouble of bothering my colleagues out in Caucasianville, bothering them with nosy questions about their case, and does she thank me? Does she? I ask you!"

"You know you'll get a week's worth of lunches out of this, so cut the crap and tell me," Helen said as she playfully punched his arm.

"Ow! You forget, I'm an old man now. Stuck driving a desk downtown. Okay, okay." He stretched his legs out, leaned back against the cushions and closed his eyes as he began to recite. "Sorry it's not more exciting, *amigo*. Melinda Wright, aged thirty-two, C.P.A. from Cal, worked at a series of respectable firms in San Francisco before going off on her own as a consultant. She specialized in stuff like this — trusts, real estate deals, wills, people with bucks. No slouch, either. She was quite well known, respected."

"Boyfriends? Girlfriends? Family?"

"Nothing. Nada. Zip. She was so fucking clean she squeaked. Mom is out in Maine, flying in tonight, Dad died while she was in college. Only child." Manny opened his eyes and his head lolled over as he looked at Helen. "Unbelievable. She lived for her work, you know? I mean, really lived for it."

Helen recalled the tight-lipped, prim woman on Jill's sofa last night. "Yeah, I can believe it. You should have seen her last night."

"Somebody did. For the last time."

"Right." Helen got up, cradling her cat in her arms, and paced around the room. Boobella purred vigorously against her throat. The cat's clean fur smelled like rain and autumn. Poor Melinda Wright. All they'd remember about her was that she was a good accountant. "What about the weapon? Any word yet?"

"Well, just like you thought, nothing found at the scene. They think it was that old favorite we all know and love, a thirty-eight special."

"Probably ended up in the creek," Helen muttered.

Manny shrugged and twisted the cap back onto the bottle of scotch. "Nothing turned up anywhere along the frontage road or in the water so far. The rain got too hard to keep slogging around in the mud, though."

"And I'm sure the paint was the same kind used in the vandalism."

"You got it." Manny sighed, heaved himself up and stretched, yawning hugely. "Looks like it came down exactly the way you thought it did, Helen. Someone up close, two shots in the back of the head when the victim tried to escape. She never had a chance."

"Now, of course, the big question is, was it the pro-life fanatics?" Helen sighed, set the cat down, followed Manny into the kitchen carrying the scotch. "This is going to be a lot of fun. At least I get to be out of the rain tomorrow morning."

"You're going to that meeting?" Manny asked as he set their empty glasses in the sink.

"I wouldn't miss it for the world! All that good fellowship and getting right with God and reporters! It'll be a change from freezing my fanny off out there in front of the clinic, scaring the patients and clinic staff to death."

Manny leaned both hands against the sink. Helen noticed the increase of gray edging in over his temples, the movie-star looks that were just barely starting to soften with time and gravity, the way his belt pulled just a tad too tight over his widening waistline. "What's up, Manny? You okay?"

"I was wondering, Helen, what do you really feel about abortion? I mean, I know it's your case right now to fake it with these guys and get to the bottom of it, but what do you really think?"

Helen gazed at him as he stared into her sink. This was not a prelude to a silly joke. Not this time. "It's not so much abortion itself I have strong feelings about, Manny. It's a question of a woman's right to determine her own life. To choose how she wants to live. I'm not so much for abortion as I am in favor of that right for all women."

"And what is that supposed to mean?" Helen drew back, startled at the anger seeping into Manny's voice. "What about the babies? Are you saying they're not human until they come out of the mother? They're a thing?"

"Hey, slow down! What's going on here?"

Manny stood up, ran a hand over his forehead and faced her. "It's just — well, things have been happening lately."

"What things? Manny, what things?"

"I mean, I got three kids of my own, and God knows I love each and every one of them — Laurie and I have been so lucky. So blessed, really. Even little Jaime. He's only three now, and he was totally unexpected." Manny smiled crookedly. "They say the surprise kids are the ones you love the most, you know? That's sure true about the little bastard."

Helen folded her arms and leaned against the counter. "Manny, what are you trying to say?"

He kept his face down as he walked to the front door. "Laurie's pregnant again. Can you believe that? Here we both are, pushing forty, and now this —"

He swallowed his words and stopped, his hand on the doorknob. "You know, I thought I knew what I believed. Now I'm not so sure. It's different, when it's your baby."

Helen stared after him for a long time before turning out the lights and going to bed.

Chapter Eight

At least, Helen thought, *these pews are padded.* A far cry from the church she went to as a kid. She could still feel the hard, rough wooden benches in the white brick meeting house, see the plain wooden cross over the communion bench that resembled someone's outcast coffee table. In this church, lighting was used to good effect over the baptistery, unlike the tableau in Helen's memory, where a homemade cotton curtain was all that separated the baptismal pool from the congregation. No cardboard fans here, either, with their funeral home ads and booster photos of the high school football teams.

Enough of memory lane. Helen sighed and dragged her thoughts to the present. Certainly the central air and heating would have been a welcome addition to the little church in Mississippi. Looking out the narrow windows set along the walls into the foggy murk of an autumn morning in Lafayette, Helen was grateful for the warm air rushing over the congregation, caressing her shoulders and feet. She unzipped her parka, looking around carefully.

Donna beamed at Helen from her seat in the pew in front of the detective. "Isn't this great? I haven't seen so many people here since last Easter! Praise the Lord!" she said in a loud whisper. Beside her, Donna's grim-faced fiancé, introduced to Helen as Gary Gordon, nodded with a satisfied expression, patting Donna's hand. Helen found it hard to stop staring at him. His face was somehow out of proportion. Broad, round and pale, with the dark shadows left by a heavy beard, Gary's nose and eyes and mouth seemed too small for his face. He stared back at Helen with eyes no bigger than raisins on a plain of pale flesh.

"About time some of these backsliders started showing up again." He adjusted his windbreaker that had his name etched over the moving company's logo and squeezed Donna's hand. "Lots of new faces, too."

Helen agreed, noting how the daily regulars who faithfully showed up to tote picket signs and pass out brochures for unwed mothers had bunched near the front, filling the first four rows of pews in the center of the church. To either side, and in back of the pro-life demonstrators, a huge crowd pushed and jostled for seats in a most un-Christian manner. The protesters, calm and even complacent in their places of honor, sat quietly, Bibles in laps beneath folded hands. In the background, from the choir loft at the back of the church, an organ with heavy vibrato hummed deep throaty tones over the rows of the curious and the faithful.

The walls of the church were lined with tall, narrow windows, some plated with stained glass, others with clear. From her vantage point, Helen could see across the side of the church to the cemetery where it sprawled across a series of low, rolling hills. The tombstones closest to the church, enclosed in a chain-link fence that seemed to have no end, dripped yesterday's rain onto the patches of green dispersed amongst the varying levels of earth. Farther on, Helen knew, the older graves stretched out in uneven rows across the underside of Lafayette, like a bedraggled petticoat that had seen better days.

Lined up in front of the cemetery the reporters pushed one another with a bit more vigor and boldness than the crowd in the church displayed. Helen could hear their muffled curses through the walls. A couple of shouting matches had started and finished as they waited for Dr. Logan to emerge from the vestry, and she could hear the click of cameras in use behind her in the vestibule. Helen risked a backward glance. It was standing-room-only, and she would bet that a good portion of the congregation hadn't come to pray.

Just as she turned around Dr. Logan emerged, his wife in attendance, beaming and smiling, even waving at a few friends in the pews. Right behind them

Dave Linville stepped out gingerly, moving as if the floor was ready to give out from under him. Helen felt a passing moment of sympathy for the suave executive, who was definitely a fish out of water in a crowd like this. And what he hoped to achieve she couldn't fathom.

"Praise the Lord, Brother Logan!"

"Amen!"

"Hallelujah!"

"As for me and my house we will serve the Lord!"

"Come, Holy Spirit, and kindle our hearts!"

At least no one was speaking in tongues yet. The reporters would have a marvelous time with that.

Amazingly enough, the noise stopped abruptly. Helen supposed everyone was too eager to hear what was about to come down to keep up the chatter. Dr. Logan and Dave Linville sat on the dais behind the communion bench, in high-backed Victorian chairs that faced the congregation. Small though he was, Logan looked right at home. This was his turf, these people were his. Dave sat awkwardly, leaning his elbows on the narrow armrests, his eyes fixed on some point at the back of the church over everyone's heads.

Mrs. Logan tiptoed to her place on the front pew as her husband smiled out at the gathered crowd. "Thank you all so much for coming out here today. I believe we should start with a prayer — a prayer for Miss Melinda Wright, who so tragically lost her life on Monday night at the hands of a cruel and godless murderer. Like the blood of Abel, may her blood cry out to our heavenly Father, who said that vengeance was His."

Dave looked extremely uncomfortable at this, but he bowed his head and screwed his eyes shut amidst the murmurs and sighs of the congregation.

"Dear Lord..." Dr. Logan began sonorously. Helen lifted her eyes and surreptitiously glanced around. In the pew in front of her, Donna's eyes were tight shut, her face a study in beatific wonder, as her lips moved soundlessly. At her side, Gary had covered his face with both hands and was completely still.

Shushing and whispering carried on at the back of the church, but Logan's prayer kept it to a minimum. Flashbulbs popped, and outside cars came and went with much whining of tires and brakes. Movement from the window caught Helen's attention once again, and she was startled to see a tall skinny kid pressed up to the narrow pane.

Cam didn't seem to notice her. His breath fogged the glass, then he turned around to shout something at the kids Helen could see gathered behind him. When he moved away from the window, Helen got a good look at one of his companions. It was Gabi, still wearing jeans and sweatshirt, though the baseball cap was gone this morning.

"In Jesus' name we ask this. Amen." A wave of amens flowed over the room. Helen leaned over to whisper to Donna as the people settled down in their pews.

"It's really stuffy in here — too many people, I think. I need a breath of air."

Rapt in the Dr. Logan's speech, Donna nodded absently. Grateful she'd managed to sit at the end of her pew, Helen walked out as quietly as possible.

"Now, Dave, I know you would like to address

these good people about the work your clinic does."
His voice, amplified by speakers spaced throughout
the building, echoed behind Helen as she slipped in
the direction of the bathrooms. The reporters and
photographers were too intent on what the minister
was saying to notice when Helen opened a door in
the vestibule that led to a service closet which in
turn opened out into the church grounds.

Breathing deeply of the fresh air — it really *had*
been stuffy in there — Helen saw Cam, Gabi and
three other kids trooping off through the rows of cars
lining the grounds in the direction of the cemetery.
Hopefully, if they spotted her they'd think she was
just another curious bystander who'd strayed from
the church. Keeping a good distance, Helen was
grateful for the thick fog. It shrouded the graves,
clinging like damp cloth to pockets of space created
by rows of granite monuments. The kids wove a
crooked path through the newest graves, stepping
between the simpering cherubs and gaudy pillars and
heaped wreaths of dying flowers. After about a
quarter of a mile on a rambling flagged path, Helen
saw them cross a long ridge into the older section of
the cemetery.

Some other time she'd have to come back and
study the place, Helen promised herself. There were
one or two markers that dated back to the 1800s.
Most of the graves were marked only by the simplest
of stones, and it was disturbing to see so many of
them mounted over dead children.

Cam and his entourage had disappeared behind a
mausoleum that was encircled by a tall iron fence
with a padlocked gate. A small signboard announced
that the Wilson Family was undertaking repairs on

their family burial plot and asked the passersby to refrain from trying to enter the unsound structure. Loose bricks, battered by the storms of the past couple of weeks, had spilled out over the sodden earth in a haphazard scatter of stone. A stream of gray cigarette smoke trailed up over the remains of the Wilsons, betraying the whereabouts of Cam and his friends.

Fortunately for Helen, the Wilsons had had the foresight to situate their mausoleum near a bank of old-growth trees that loomed over the weathered granite. She stepped quietly through the wet grass and into the cold shadows beneath the trees. The fog parted around her, then swathed the trees, covering her presence.

"Fuck you, Cam," a boy's voice whined. "I think you're full of shit, man."

"Like, you really saw the dude that did her? Quit jerking us off!"

"Hey, did I say it was a dude?" Helen recognized Cam's nasal monotone. "Look, you assholes don't have to believe me. All I'm saying is I was at our place that night, checking out all the shit there, and next thing I know there's this scream and then I heard it."

"Heard what?"

"Heard what, heard what? Jesus fucking Christ, what the fuck am I talking about here? Heard the gun, you shitface!"

"Come on, you're just shitting us, right?"

There was a long silence, then, "I can prove it," Cam said quietly.

"Yeah, right. I'd like to see you do that."

"Here." Helen heard gasps from several different

people. What the hell was the kid doing? "See? See that? I told you!"

"Fuck!"

Was it the gun? Helen strained to listen, but an awed quiet had fallen over the group. Damn it, why didn't they say something? she fumed.

What she heard next, though, was not Cam and his friends. Shouts were coming out of the church, and it didn't sound like ecstatic prayer.

"Come on, we gotta split," Cam said. Helen saw them slipping on the grass as they climbed the ridge and disappeared further into the cemetery. She was torn between following them and going back to the church, then decided that the better course was to head back to her coterie of demonstrators. Cam no doubt knew his way around the cemetery as if it were his own backyard — he'd have all sorts of hiding places and escape routes that would leave Helen far behind in the fog.

She hurried over the ridge in the opposite direction, back to where the shouting came from. News vans had rolled up almost to the entrance of the church, and the police had arrived.

Helen saw a wave of people pushing their way through the church entrance, some faces red with fury, others pale and distraught, a few even glowing with excitement that was almost sexual. One man stood, arms folded and legs straddled firmly on the stone steps leading up to the church, talking to a reporter whose microphone bobbed near the man's face.

Helen recognized Gary staring into the video equipment, speaking calmly, his out-of-balance features taut with anger. "There's a bunch of us, all brothers in the Lord," he was saying to the camera, "who think that maybe these vandals have the right idea, you know? Maybe these baby killers need to get a taste of their own. I mean, here they are, killing poor, innocent, defenseless human beings, so maybe they should be treated the same way, you know?"

"Are you saying, Mr. — Mr. —"

"Gordon. Gary Gordon."

"Mr. Gordon, are you saying that these people who work at the clinic deserve to die?" The reporter could hardly contain himself at the scent of a sizzling sound bite.

"All I'm saying is that it's right there in the Bible. An eye for an eye, and a tooth for a tooth." He blinked his raisin eyes at the lights going off from cameras that suddenly surrounded him. "Jesus said that if anyone offended one of these little ones they ought to be thrown into the sea with a stone around their necks. Now, to me, that sounds like an order to carry out punishment."

"Amen, brother!"

"Give 'em hell, Gary, that's what they asked for!"

"The man speaks the truth, it's in the Bible!"

Standing demurely behind him, Donna smiled broadly, starry-eyed with devotion and pride. She looked at the people gathering around her fiancé, spotted Helen and waved.

"Now this Dave Linville, he's walking into God's house and saying before God that the Linville Clinic does community service. Right in front of God he lies! He stands there and tries to cover over his sin, but it *will* be found out!"

The cheers encouraged him, and Gary's voice increased in depth and carrying power. "I say, let the

Lord's will be done! I say, we don't have to put up with this evil taking over our women and children! Who will go with me? Who will follow me to that den of Satan and strike a blow for Jesus?"

The rest of his words were drowned out as cheers and something close to a rebel yell streamed out from the knot of people clustered around. Helen saw them racing for their cars. All over the church grounds engines roared. Gary and Donna, in Gary's pickup, were the first to tear off down the curving drive that led to Mt. Diablo Boulevard, tires smoking as they led the way to the clinic.

"Oh, my Lord, my Lord." Behind her, Dr. Logan ignored the shouts of reporters and stood sadly with a skimpy group of stragglers who'd chosen to remain at the church. Dave Linville, hunched sheepishly in the background, tried to be invisible just inside the doors of the church.

No one involved with the media wanted to stay behind and talk to Dr. Logan. The news vans wheeled swiftly out, taking up the rear of the caravan, spitting out gravel and exhaust as they disappeared beyond the trees.

"Dr. Logan, I don't know what to say. I — I had no idea this would happen. I can't believe these people wouldn't listen to you."

"Son, if you knew as much about human nature as I do, after forty years of ministry, you'd know to expect the unexpected." Dr. Logan went to Dave's side and patted him on the shoulder. "It wasn't your fault. These people have their blood up, they're so fired up about what they see as immoral." He sighed, shook his head and looked around the entrance. "Honey? Honey, I think we'd better get on over to the clinic. Maybe I can get them to settle down over there."

Helen stood alone with Dave on the stone steps. "What the hell happened in there?"

Dave shook his head and stared out at the empty parking lot. "Hell if I know. All I did was talk about the different programs the clinic offered, try to get them to see that the Linville does so much more than abortions. They just didn't give a damn, Helen. They weren't there to listen to anything. Not even from poor old Logan."

Helen nodded. "You're right. They didn't want words. They wanted blood." With a sigh she walked to her car. "I'm going to the clinic."

Chapter Nine

The sun broke through the fog and clouds, bathing the white stone of the clinic with soft light. Helen turned her face up toward the sky, enjoying the sudden warmth. Summer and winter in California were always so predictable — summer was hot and dry, winter was damp and chill. The other seasons, though, were completely out of kilter. It was never possible to determine what weird turn the climate might take. This morning promised to be un- seasonably hot.

With a grateful sigh, Helen took off her jacket

and tied it into a thick awkward knot around her waist. The wind had died, and the last traces of mist dissipated, steaming from the top of her car.

It had proven impossible to park next to the clinic. Helen found a side street that curled back away from the freeway, parallel to the frontage road where Melinda had been found. Slogging through the mud at the edge of the street, Helen was working up a sweat under the brilliant sunlight.

Even if she hadn't known where the Linville was, all she had to do was follow the hollering and yelling coming from the other side of the fence. As she rounded the side of the clinic, Helen ran up against a wall of people. There was no way she'd be able to make her way through this.

"Helen! Over here!" Somehow in this mess Donna had spotted her and was waving frantically. Gary stopped in the middle of his speech, given from the flatbed of his pickup, as Donna beckoned her on.

She shouldered her way as cautiously as she could, surprised at how the crowd split and broke around her. Maybe she gained in prestige because the private property of the saint of the hour — meaning, of course, Donna — had greeted her alone out of the throng.

Whatever the reason, Helen was apprehensive of joining the couple on the truck. She climbed up and sat down on the metal hub that covered the rear wheel, listening to Gary spout more incendiary bullshit. Dave was nowhere to be seen, and Dr. Logan stood mournfully in front of the pickup, his glasses reflecting the sun back up at Gary.

Rather than listen any longer, Helen watched the crowd. She was relieved to note that at least half the gathering consisted of reporters and photographers. And she wasn't at all sure that the faithful followers were all that ready to storm the Linville's battlements and destroy Satan and all his works inside.

In fact, Gary's eloquence was fading fast. He faltered, screwed up a couple of quotes from the scriptures, and finally started praying in a loud voice.

Dr. Logan knelt, wincing as his old knees met the gravel, but clearly grateful that the crowd was taking a peaceful turn. Helen watched his lips move in silent prayer. She didn't doubt for a moment that his pleas to God were completely different from those Gary offered.

The people stood still, with bowed heads or uplifted hands. As Gary finished, someone broke into a hymn, one of the more lugubrious ones Helen remembered from childhood, full of descriptions of a saccharine heaven peopled by Technicolor cherubs and fluttery harp music. Still, it was a vast improvement from the bloodbath Gary had tried to begin.

At the edge of the crowd, Helen saw her. Allison stood quietly, waiting by the rows of cars, perhaps letting the prayer end before trying to move through the people. Was she getting thinner? Maybe those bags under her eyes were just a trick of the light, but Helen didn't like how tense and exhausted she looked. When this was all over and done with, vandals arrested, demonstrations stopped and murderers safely behind bars, Helen was definitely going to have to come back to the Linville. Maybe she could put in some time as a volunteer, too. Hell, she'd been feeling guilty for years now about not doing anything for the community, so —

Dr. Logan stood up and Gary helped him up into

the truck. The people shifted, and Helen watched as Allison slowly picked her way to the entrance of the clinic, edging around the sides near the grass.

Allison smiled — at first Helen thought that the smile was meant for her — then she turned around to see Bud waving at her. He looked a bit pale, and his eyes were watchful, but other than that he stood like the same stalwart monolith Helen always saw standing guard. He moved away from the entrance to help Allison up the steps.

That was when it happened. At first, Helen wasn't sure she'd seen anything, really. A sudden flash of movement, a glint from the sun. Allison put her hand up to her head and frowned. She stopped and turned to face the crowd with a puzzled expression on her face.

They continued up the steps, then there was another odd movement. Allison looked up sharply, and Helen saw a trickle of red streaked over her eyebrow.

Following Allison's gaze, Helen saw him standing in the middle of the gathering. She was surprised she hadn't noticed him before. Had he been at the church? Or was he waiting for Allison here at the clinic?

"Oh, my God," she heard Allison yell. "Bob. It's Bob."

The man Allison called Bob stretched to his full height. Over the past two days he'd neglected to shave, and a dark stubble fuzzed his chin and cheeks. Bob lifted his shaking hands, filled with stones, his eyes burning with rage.

"You damned bitch! Go to hell!" His hand moved

swiftly, and a stone flew across the truck, hitting Allison on the shoulder.

That was all Gary needed. "Yes, brother! Just like Jesus throwing the money changers from the temple!"

The crowd muttered, the energy shifted, and Helen felt anger rising again.

"Are we here to do the Lord's work today?"

"Yes, Brother Gary!" a few voices cried out.

"Are we going to strike a mortal blow to Satan?"

"Amen!"

"Do we have the power of the Lord on our side, brothers and sisters?"

The crowd screamed as one voice in response, and suddenly the pickup rocked back and forth as people rushed forward, spilling over the walkway toward the clinic entrance. Dr. Logan was completely ignored, his pleas swallowed up in the confused shouts of people who only moments ago had been quietly praying and singing. Gary played them like his own private orchestra. Mimicking Bob, he jumped down and gathered gravel in his hands, showing his ammunition to the mob.

"Let's follow Jesus into battle!" he cried out. Donna, her face contorted with wild passion, screamed something unintelligible as she followed Gary.

Helen watched with horror as several other men and women picked up rocks from the heaps of gravel, some hesitantly, most with eager abandon, weighing and sorting to find the biggest ones.

Bud unfroze and pulled Allison with him to the doors. Just as it looked like he'd made it to safety, however, several pairs of arms reached up, pulling him nearly off his feet and grabbing for his sidearm. In the tussle, Allison lost her hold on Bud's arm and fell over, in danger of being trampled.

Helen sprang out of the pickup and in two strides made it to Allison's side. With a glance over her shoulder, she spotted Bob. He was immobile in the midst of the crowd, struggling to break loose and make his way to his target. Helen saw his eyes blaze, fixed on the woman at her side.

"Come on, we've got to get you out of here!" Helen tugged at Allison, pulling her along, as Bud scrambled back to his feet. Hands came out from the doorway and got him inside. "Damnit, now!"

Allison wiped blood from her forehead and stumbled along behind Helen. Bob was making progress in breaking loose from the stranglehold of the mob, but Helen and Allison were closer to freedom than he was. The angry protesters were fixated on the clinic, so no one tried to stop Helen from leaving the area. She hurried along the side of the parking lot, coaxing Allison along, aware that the blow from the rocks may have seriously injured her.

By the time they made it to the frontage road, Helen began to breathe a little easier. Bob hadn't emerged from the clinic area yet, and Helen's car was only a short walk away.

She stopped to look at Allison. "We'd better get you to a doctor," she said. "That cut might be serious."

"No. No, I said!" Allison broke free of Helen's grasp, then stumbled, nearly falling down into the grass. "Just leave me alone, will you? There is nothing wrong with me. I'm fine."

"Yeah, sure you are." Helen gently helped her up.

"Steady, now. Don't try to hurry. We'll get where we're going."

"And where is that?" Allison protested, although she quit pushing Helen away. Helen felt Allison's weight on her shoulder as she leaned into Helen. She was completely oblivious to what that sensation was doing to Helen.

"Well, if you don't want to go to the doctor, how about home? Do you live here in Lafayette?"

Allison froze, stiffening against Helen's arm. "No. No, I can't go there. Bob might show up there. Oh, Christ, I don't know what to do."

"A friend's house?"

Allison burst out in a short, sharp laugh, then wavered, touching her forehead gingerly. "In this town? I don't have friends here. Not anymore."

Helen sighed, looked behind them. The coast was still clear, but they needed to get out fast. Then it hit her. "Look," she said, walking them around the bend in the road that hid her car from view. "I know this café here — it's bound to be pretty quiet. Maybe we could sit down, have a cup of coffee? Figure out what to do next?"

By now they had reached the car. Helen unlocked the passenger door and opened it, but Allison backed off.

"Wait. What's your name?"

"Helen. It's Helen."

"Okay. Now I can get in." Confused, Helen watched as Allison slid onto the seat, then leaned back on the headrest, wincing in pain.

"What the hell was that all about?" Helen asked, amused and puzzled, as she turned the car around back to the main street.

"Well, I never get into cars with strangers. Now you're not a stranger, Helen. Even if you *are* a pro-life right-wing fanatic."

Helen smiled. Now what the fuck was she supposed to do? Suddenly, in spite of all that had happened, in spite of Melinda's death, in spite of Frieda and Jill, Helen felt happy. With a shock she realized she hadn't felt this lighthearted in months.

"Actually, I might surprise you."

"Oh, yeah? Meaning you suddenly saw the light and registered Democrat?"

"I've been a card-carrying member of the Greens for a long time. No, that wasn't what I meant."

As they drove by the Linville, Helen glimpsed the familiar blue and red flash of police cars. "The media is going to really love this," she said, hoping to get Allison to smile again.

"Slow down a minute, please?" Allison asked in a quavering voice. Helen obliged, hoping Allison wouldn't get out of the car. But all she did was peer carefully through the crowd. "Okay, let's go," she muttered. "I didn't see him."

"You mean Bob?"

Allison turned to look at Helen. "What — oh, damn, that hurt! Shit," and her hand flew back to her forehead. "Just go slow for a while, okay? Now, what were you going to say?"

Helen tried to keep her eyes off Allison as she stretched out more comfortably in the passenger's seat. She was awfully thin, Helen noticed, and she looked like she could use a year of sleep. But her hair gleamed in the sunlight, and the profile limned against the window was delicate, with clean precise lines and soft full lips.

"What exactly did you see out there?"

Helen described the scene at the clinic, careful to delete her own activities up to the moment she'd rushed Allison to safety. "Who is he? Boyfriend?" Helen asked, steeling herself for the answer.

"Hardly. Bob is — we've been divorced for two years now. I haven't seen him for those two years until today."

Helen turned off into another side street that was little more than an alley. After three blocks, the lanes opened out into a wide drive that spiraled around a traffic circle. The signboard that read JAVA JONES swung gently back and forth in the breeze, the small rainbow in the corner of the sign shining in the sun.

"Here we are."

Allison climbed out of the car and squinted up at the row of gleaming windows. "I didn't know this place was here," she said as she walked inside with Helen.

"It hasn't been open for long," Helen said. "The owner is an old friend of mine." Helen decided not to add that years ago she and Ramona, proprietor and chef of Java Jones, had once dated a few times. It had never gotten further than a couple of kisses, but Helen knew first-hand what a great cook Ramona was.

"Helen! It's about time! I was just telling Darcy the other day that we haven't seen you in here for ages. How's it going?" Ramona broke off her greeting as she looked at Allison. The dark-haired woman, her curly brown hair gleaming and her well-toned body slim and taut under the cover of an apron, hurried out from behind the counter. "What happened?"

"She got hit in the head with a rock."

"What? Hey, Darcy, could you bring out some water?" Moments later, after Helen reassured Ramona that no lawsuits would come from it, Helen was cautiously dabbing peroxide on Allison's forehead with a cotton ball.

"You're going to have a pretty nasty bruise," she said as she capped the peroxide and set it on the counter.

"Well, I'll just tell people they should see the other guy."

Helen smiled, until she saw Allison's eyes fill with tears.

"Yeah," she repeated, "the other guy. Why the hell did he have to come back here?" She took a sip of water, struggled for composure and smiled back at Helen. "Sorry. Allison Young."

Helen took her proffered hand. "Now I guess it's okay for me to ride in a car with you, too." She realized too late that she was holding Allison's hand far too long and let go sheepishly. "How's the head?"

"Oh, I think I'll live. Thanks." She accepted the coffee from Ramona, and Helen deliberately avoided the interested look Ramona sent their way. "So, you want to tell me what this is about?"

"What are you talking about?" Helen asked, her stomach tightening with a sensation of nausea. *Now what?*

"You've been out there with those religious fanatics for a couple of weeks, watching everything like a hawk. Watching me, if I'm not completely off track." Allison leaned forward, holding the cotton ball to her forehead. "What's going on here?"

Helen sighed, leaned back in the chair. "Could I have one, too, Ramona?" she called back towards the kitchen. Allison watched her expectantly. "This may take a while."

Chapter Ten

By the time Helen and Allison had pulled up into Helen's driveway in Berkeley, it was dark. "Are you sure you don't want me to take you back to Lafayette, Allison?" Helen had asked repeatedly on the drive to her house.

"Not tonight. I can't go back there. You don't know — what might be waiting for me there."

Who, Helen had silently corrected her. "So why did your ex-husband suddenly reappear? You said he'd been gone for two years."

Helen tried not to stare and fuss over the cut on

Allison's forehead. Actually, it did look much better — the peroxide had done its work, and Helen could see that the tear in her skin really wasn't deep. The bruise was going to be an ugly one. With the car pointed west, they'd headed directly toward the setting sun, and Allison shielded her eyes from the glare, wincing. "Quit staring at me, Helen. I'm fine."

That had been three hours ago. Now Allison was making friends with Boobella, who piteously proclaimed her sorrowful state of neglect and starvation. "Hey, I had cats, too, you know? Lighten up, kitty, I know when I'm being lied to." Allison hoisted the cat onto her lap and Boobella melted into what Helen called "kitty meditation" — flat on her back, legs spread wide, soft belly available to be rubbed.

Helen gathered up the empty Chinese food cartons from the coffee table. This was much too comfortable. She really ought to get Allison back to her own home.

As she was trying to come up with a polite way to say it, Allison remarked, "This was really sweet, Helen. I can't tell you how glad I am to be out of that God-awful house." She sighed and looked around her. "I love places like this — older, lots of character, really homey and lived in."

"You mean that recently-visited-by-a-tornado look. I'm so glad you appreciate it. I really had to work hard to achieve this effect."

Allison laughed. Helen felt warmed at the sound. It was the first time she'd heard her laughing. "Believe me, it's better than the showroom effect. That's the way Bob wanted it, the whole five years we were together."

Helen picked up her mug of hot tea and spiked a dollop of brandy into it. It was just the right temperature to drink now. "Why do you keep staying there, Allison?"

"Obviously you haven't looked at the real estate market lately. I've only just now heard from a buyer who sounds like he means it. It'll be good to get out of there."

"Won't you miss it? I mean, you've been in Lafayette for several years."

Allison picked up a chopstick and began to toy with it over Boobella's head. She smiled as the cat tried to bat the slender stick with her paws. "I meant it when I said that I don't have friends there. I'm — well, I don't exactly fit in with the moms driving kids to swim meets and baking for the chamber of commerce street fair. You've been there, watching the place for your investigation. You've seen what it's like. Fit in, or else."

"Yes, there is that, but — it's odd. As far as the right-wing pro-life faction, at least." Quit worrying, she told herself. It's just conversation. You're not revealing anything important to the case. Just because she has such pretty hair, and those eyes — "I mean," she went on, "they do have standards they consider normal, but I also think they act out of ignorance. And what they don't understand, they fear. And what they fear, they attack."

Allison nodded. "Yeah, I think you're right about their motivation. Don't get me wrong, Helen. When I got married, I thought that was exactly what I wanted — what I was born for." She sighed and let Boobella take over on the chopstick, letting it fall directly into her waiting paws. "Have you ever been through that — thought you knew yourself, knew how you wanted to live your life, then had it all just blown out of the water?"

Helen stood up, holding the cartons, ready to take them into the kitchen. Anything to get away from those green eyes that were even now blinking back tears. "It's what I'm famous for, Allison. That, and saving damsels in distress, of course."

It was no use. Allison slid out from under a very disappointed cat and followed Helen into the kitchen. "This is awful. Here I am, taking advantage of how nice you are, babbling away. I wish you'd let me clean up."

"There's nothing to do. That's the beauty of take-out." Helen flipped the containers into the garbage can under the sink. "See? Dishes are done."

Allison suddenly put her hands up to her face. Her shoulders quivered with silent weeping.

"Hey, don't cry. My jokes aren't that bad, are they? Come on, let's go back into the living room."

"I know what you're probably thinking of me —"

"Christ, I hope not," Helen muttered as she led Allison back to the sofa.

"What?"

"Nothing. You're not a weak or bad person because you're afraid to go back to your house, Allison. Bob Young is dangerous. You're wise to avoid him."

Allison got up and began to prowl around the room, idly picking up and then putting down odd objects scattered around the room — pieces from a collection of seashells, a pile of paperbacks, one lone silver hoop earring resting by an ashtray, a lacquered box. "Were you ever married, Helen?"

"Not to a man." Was that what this was all about? A way to pass the time by picking the brains and heart of the nearest new "thing"? Getting in on what was supposed to be the latest fad? No, Helen decided. Allison's fear was real. Her being in Helen's house had nothing to do with the fact that she'd just told Allison, only hours ago, that she was a lesbian.

"But — you've lived with someone?"

"Yes. A couple of someones, in fact. And although some of my relationships have had abusive aspects, I've never experienced what you have."

"It's like never waking up from a nightmare." Allison stopped prowling and settled down on a pile of oversized pillows by the television, gripping her mug of hot tea firmly with both hands, her eyes huge and fixed on the wall opposite. "The whole year we were separated, before the divorce was final, I never knew when I'd turn around and see him there. Not doing anything, not saying anything — just staring, so full of hate he could barely stand up. It felt like ice and fire all at once, the way he looked at me."

"You must have gone to court, gotten restraining orders —"

Allison snorted and turned to Helen with a grimace of disgust. "Oh, yeah, that was a real big help. They're all the same, these — these *men,* who sit there and make decisions about my life and what's best for me. They're all part of the same gentlemen's club, you know? If you scratch my back, I'll scratch yours. I can't even begin to describe the way the judge sat in that courtroom and laughed —" She broke off and hissed in pain, her fingers carefully searching the cut on her head. "Jesus, remind me not to get upset for a few weeks, okay?" She sat very still, eyes closed, leaning against the wall.

"Maybe you ought to lie down for a while." Helen got up and moved quietly across the room. Intending to help her to the sofa she touched Allison's arm.

Allison started. "Sorry. I didn't hear you coming."

"Next time I'll knock." She was kneeling beside her, drinking in those cool green eyes. "Is that cut bleeding again?" she said softly, leaning closer.

"I don't think so." Allison spoke in a whisper, and Helen stroked her hair back from the cut. "Guess I'm a little jumpy."

They stayed in that position for what felt like eternity. Helen tried to sort out her feelings quickly and get them out of the way. Damnit, she'd been in this situation before — a straight woman who either knows exactly what kind of fire she's playing with, or one who hasn't a clue what sort of messages she's sending out to any self-respecting dyke. Helen fought to ignore the way Allison's full lips parted, her breath bathing Helen's skin with warmth.

"Look, maybe you could go into the bedroom, and I'll stretch out on the sofa. We've both had enough excitement for one day, and —"

"Shut up, Helen." Allison laced her fingers behind Helen's neck and pulled her close, close, until their lips touched. Helen sank into the kiss, knowing all along that it might be deadly poison, not caring how much it might hurt later on. In the back of her throat Allison was making soft moaning sounds, which only drove Helen to kiss her deeper, harder.

"Oh, God, it's been so long, Helen." Allison's whisper burned Helen's ear as Helen stroked the soft skin of Allison's neck with her tongue. She could feel the pulse in Allison's throat, the quickening of the woman's blood with each caress. Allison's hands loosened their hold on Helen's neck, and she began to knead Helen's back.

With a deep sigh, Helen arched her back, pressing herself forward until breast touched breast, the soft pressure of warm flesh rising to meet her. Tension surged between Helen's legs. Suddenly nervous, she pulled away. "Look, Allison, I know you've had a hell of a day, and maybe you'd rather think about this before —"

"I thought I told you to shut up." Another kiss stopped Helen before she could protest any further. As she slowly unbuttoned Helen's shirt, Allison started to giggle. "Did you think you were the only one with eyes in your head out there at the clinic? Every day I was there, for three weeks, you stood there watching. Not shouting, not praying or cursing — watching."

Helen almost gasped when Allison's hands stroked her nipples. The warmth of her palms contrasting with the chill in the room excited her. "And here I thought I was being so good at my job, detecting my freezing ass off."

"I'm betting you're very, very good at what you do." Allison slipped a cushion under Helen's back as she gently pushed her flat on the floor. "Let's find out, shall we?"

Helen quit fighting when Allison's mouth grazed her breasts, her warm wet tongue coaxing the nipples to harden. Long cool fingers unzipped Helen's jeans and began to explore the soft curly hair below her belly. Helen's body, denied for many months, responded quickly as the fingers plunged into her, probing deep inside for the most sensitive spots. Helen thrust her hips back and forth, her excitement mounting to a swift climax.

"Jesus," she breathed, opening her eyes to see Allison smiling down at her. Sweat tunneled between her breasts and her jeans were soaked. "I'm not usually so — so fast."

"Seems to me like someone was ready." Allison pulled her shirt off over her head, her soft hair settling around her bare shoulders.

Helen adjusted the pillows beneath her head as Allison slipped out of her slacks and straddled her. Eagerly she supported Allison's hips and lowered her down. Helen's tongue laved the sweet flesh lined with thick curly hair, parting the folds of skin to find the tiny bump that hardened and enlarged with each rocking motion.

"Yes, Helen, yes," Allison moaned. Her hips moved faster and faster, bearing down. Matching Allison's thrusts, Helen slid two fingers in and out, in and out, until Allison cried out above her, her whole body shuddering with her orgasm. With a tremulous sigh, Allison moved off of Helen and lay next to her on the floor. "God, that was great," she moaned. "I'm not sure I can move."

Helen felt something warm and furry next to her head and turned around to get a face full of Boobella's fur. The cat hopped over Helen and nestled next to Allison. "I think we have company. Boobella, your sense of timing sucks big-time."

Laughing, Allison got up, grabbed her clothes and

strode naked across the room. "I wonder if maybe there's anything like a bed in this house. What do you think?"

Helen came up behind her, Boobella skittering ahead. "You mean blankets and a mattress and everything?"

"Just like uptown." They landed on Helen's bed and scuttled beneath the pile of quilts and blankets, cuddling close in the darkness. Helen was surprised at her own happiness — here she was, making love to a woman she'd met a few hours ago, laughing and teasing and joking as if it were the most natural thing in the world.

"What is it, oh great private investigator? You look very solemn all of a sudden."

Helen looked up, unable in the darkness to see the green eyes she'd stared into with lust moments ago. "I was just thinking — who would have thought this morning, after a riot at a clinic, I'd be in bed with a beautiful woman like you?"

Allison grew very still. Helen could feel the tension creeping over her and mentally kicked herself for throwing a wet towel on this fascinating situation.

"I — I don't know what you must think of me, Helen," she said quietly. "Believe me, I don't do this. I mean, I haven't done it. Oh, fuck, I can't seem to say this right."

"Hey, no cursing in my bed. Not until I say you can." Now was not the time to worry or feel regrets or think about what would happen in the morning. Helen moved on top of Allison, warmth building again between her legs from deep inside, letting the weight of her body caress the woman lying beneath her.

"Guess I can't ask you to fuck me, then, huh?"

"You don't even have to ask." Helen kissed her hard and long. She spread her legs wide, rubbing her crotch against Allison's, pushing up against the pressure points she'd tasted not long before. This time they waited to come, drawing back from each other as the tension mounted, thrusting their hips together over and over, playing it out, groaning with pleasure and its denial.

They didn't come exactly at the same time, but it was damn close. Helen trailed Allison by moments, almost crying with the intensity of it, muffling her voice against Allison's neck.

"No, no, stay on me, Helen," Allison murmured.

Helen did, until her breathing settled down and they both shivered with cold. Moving as if drunk, Helen pulled blankets over them. Allison was asleep almost instantly. Her soft warm breath bathed Helen's shoulder as Helen lay still, not wanting to rouse her and possibly watch her get dressed and leave. Questions kept spilling into her mind, pushing sleep aside.

Later, she promised herself. Tomorrow. They could get this all talked out tomorrow. For now, she wanted to enjoy this. Sometime toward dawn Helen slept.

Chapter Eleven

"And that's when you met Bob? After you and your lover parted ways?"

Allison nodded. If anything, Helen thought, she looked even more beautiful in the morning than she had the night before. The cut over her right eye was looking much better, and the swelling near the eyebrow had gone down considerably. Tousled hair spilled into her eyes, and Allison brushed it aside frequently as she nibbled at the English muffin Helen had toasted for her.

Helen took a big bite of her own bagel and cream

cheese. At her feet, Boobella licked cheese off the small plate Helen had provided. The shards of the plate Allison had dropped earlier were safely deposited in the garbage. Fortunately the nervousness they'd both felt on getting up this morning had vanished, broken like the plate that fell from Allison's hands.

"Yes. Debbie was — well, she was just too afraid. And I had these visions of the picket fence and the dog and the station wagon, you know? Just like a good little straight white girl from the 'burbs." She smiled, gazing off somewhere into the past. "I was too naïve to imagine how any of that would happen for me without a husband. So basically I married an idea. The American woman's dream. What an ass I was."

"Hey." Helen reached across and took Allison's hand. "Don't ever kick yourself for having dreams, or for making a mistake. I'm just really sorry that that particular dream turned into such pain for you."

Allison shrugged, squeezed Helen's hand and forced a smile. "Somehow it was worse when I got possession of the house. Worse for me, I mean. I knew I didn't want it. Bob was the one who always loved it. He should have gotten it and been able to stay in Lafayette."

"But you didn't want him to have it?"

She sighed and pulled Helen's bathrobe tightly around her. "It wasn't that so much as the fact that I needed some kind of security. Or so I thought. Now it's just a fucking millstone around my neck. Thank God we didn't have kids, at least."

Helen finished her bagel and looked past Allison out the kitchen window. It was going to be much colder today — no sign of the sun that had tempted everyone with the promise of warmth yesterday afternoon.

"I probably ought to get back over to Lafayette soon."

"Oh, I'm sorry I'm keeping you." Nervous once again, Allison fussed with plates and knives and cups, quickly shuffling dishes together to pile them into the sink.

"Hey, hey, it's okay! I mean, you don't exactly have to rush, do you?" Helen asked, embracing her from behind as she stood at the sink.

"What, afraid I'll go through all your dishes?" Allison laughed as she ran the hot water, squeezing soap over the pile of crockery.

"Seriously, are you working right now? Do I need to get you back home right away?"

"No, unemployed at the moment. Although I'm looking." She stopped scrubbing and let her hands fall into the water, leaning against Helen. "Mmm, that feels perfect. Just a little lower."

Helen moved her hands farther down Allison's back, kneading the muscles just below her shoulder blades. "How's the head?"

"At the moment, fine. There's one or two other parts that could use some attention, though."

Helen pressed her face against Allison's neck. "Can we talk about what we'd like to do later? I mean, I'm not pressuring you for some kind of ultimate answer, but I'd love to see you again."

"I was just thinking," Allison said, "of a way to ask if I could come over again tonight. We could just talk, if you like."

"As long as we don't eat Chinese food." Helen laughed. "You've seen what that does to me."

Helen padded back down the hallway, Allison's laughter ringing through the house. As she began to shed her sweatsuit for jeans and sweater, Helen felt a weird twinge, a moment of pain. This would be very easy to get used to — laughter in the kitchen, a soft warm body next to her at night, a lovely woman in her life again. She closed her eyes and shut down on the longing. How could she even think along those lines? They'd met, officially, only yesterday. Allison was on the rebound from a painful and abusive divorce, probably in desperate need of comfort. That wasn't love last night, it was sex. Great sex, true, but there was no reason to —

Another crash echoed from the other end of the house. Helen smiled. Maybe she *would* have to get a new set of dishes, if Allison kept hanging around. "Hey, what was it this time? My Raiders mug?" she called.

Helen zipped up her jeans and shoved her arms through the sleeves of her sweater as she went back to the kitchen. She froze in the doorway, watching Allison huddled up as close as she could get in the corner by the pantry. Her eyes flashed with fear when Helen walked toward her.

"Look, Allison, it was just a couple of plates. Please, don't do this —"

"It wasn't. It wasn't a plate." Helen followed her eyes to the window. "Someone is out there. They — they hit something, or broke it, or I don't know — I heard it."

Helen stood close by, edging over just enough to

peer out of the window into her backyard. Gray murk covered everything, without a glimmer of sunlight to break through the fog. There was no breeze, so the mist hung still and thick over the landscaping that Helen had put in herself — the rows of fruit trees that still needed several years to produce plums and apples, the magnolia she'd spent so much money on that bloomed year-round, the second-hand patio table and chairs that sat waiting to be used.

Then she heard it again. It must have been one of the terra cotta planters she'd put out during the summer, maybe the one nearest the house that held a thriving jade plant. She'd moved it close to the back door, thinking that it would be easier to drag it into the house on cold nights. The clink of shattered clay skipped on the flagstones of the patio.

Helen put her mouth close to Allison's ear. "Wait here." With one swift motion, bent over beneath the edge of the window, Helen crept to the back door. Yes, it was firmly locked, the chain and double bolt secure. All the windows had been shut, Helen knew, against the cold last night. The house was too old to have sliding glass doors. She looked up at Allison, who was still shaking, flat against the pantry door. "Allison," she whispered, "I'm going to check the front door and grab my cell phone, then come right back here. Stay there. Okay?"

Helen stared at her until her lips moved. "Okay."

Helen nodded, then sped through the hall. Where was the damn thing, anyway? Oh, yes — over on the side table next to the lamp. Helen had left it there while unloading Chinese food last night, proud of herself for actually remembering to bring it in from the car.

As she clutched the phone, she remembered something else. The gun she hadn't carried for months lay in the locked drawer. Without thinking, Helen fumbled for the key that was hidden behind the lamp, unlocked and pulled open the drawer, grabbed the gun and a handful of ammunition from the box below the table. Bob Young is a dangerous man, she told herself. She and Allison were not safe there.

Allison. What the hell was she thinking? She didn't need a loaded gun. What she needed was to get back in the kitchen, get the police on the phone and handle the situation. And handling the situation didn't mean putting on some kind of butch show of dyke virility.

Helen carried the gun as far as the kitchen entrance, then put it down on the little shelf that held her slim collection of cookbooks just inside the doorjamb. Allison hadn't moved.

"Did you hear anything else?" Helen whispered as she punched in nine-one-one.

Suddenly she heard an enormous crash. Splinters of glass showered over her, reflecting the dull morning light as they fell around the room and onto her shoulders. Then she felt a sharp pain on the side of her head. Someone cried out, then there was a whole series of confusing noises — heavy feet pounding near the wall, a rough deep voice shouting curses. Numb darkness followed, and Helen struggled to stay conscious, fading in and out to the sound of Allison's whispered pleas.

When the room finally stopped swirling in a painful morass of color and light, and things solidified into recognizable objects, Helen figured out her position on the kitchen floor. Whatever had knocked her in the head had sent her sprawling across the room. Her head and upper body lay across the entrance to the kitchen, her feet pointed at the two people standing by the sink.

A jagged hole split open the window over the sink. Bits of glass glittered on the floor all around them, crunching with a grating sound under Bob's boots. Allison was bent backwards over the sink, as far away from Bob as she could.

"I told you, bitch," he muttered at her, "I told you I wasn't done with you yet."

"Bob, this doesn't have to go any further. You can stop anytime and get the hell out of this house —"

The neat slap shut her up quickly. Helen flinched, rage and frustration searing more pain into her muscles. Memory flooded back in with clarity, and she flexed her fingers, reaching slowly and silently for the gun she knew had to be close to her side. If she could just reach up without Bob noticing, she'd have it in her hands in moments, getting him away from Allison.

As her fingers started to crawl across the small stack of cookbooks, she froze at the sight of Bob raising her gun in his hand, pointing the muzzle at Allison's head. It was inches from her temple. Helen lowered her arm before Bob caught sight of the movement. Shit, if she could just move, she could stop this.

"How does it feel to be this close to dead, bitch? Huh? Now you know how it feels." He laughed, an ugly sharp noise, butting the pistol gently on her cut forehead. Allison winced and Helen heard a whimper escape from her lips. "You took it all away from me, and now you get it all taken from you." He clicked off the safety, grinning. "You got the house, you got to stay there. Me, I got nothing. Well, guess what? Time to pay up!"

Helen lay flat, flexing her legs, gauging distances. If she could move fast enough, she'd be able to kick one of the kitchen chairs across the floor and distract him enough to get Allison out of the room. She froze when glass shards underneath her back slithered and scraped on the linoleum, but Bob paid no attention.

Allison had, amazingly enough, begun to laugh. "Right, Bob! It's all my fault that you're such a miserable son of a bitch."

He panted, confused. "Shut the fuck up, cunt!"

"Yeah, I'm the one that lost job after job. I'm the one who went through our savings with expensive cars and watches and remodeling. It was me that cashed in the retirement funds, even forging my own signature on loan papers. Yep, you've got it right!"

"I ought to just shoot you right now —"

"And I broke my own ribs three years ago, didn't I? Oh, yeah, and that dislocated shoulder — that was me, going out there and twisting myself up, getting off on all that pain!" Allison stood straight, facing Bob with only a couple of inches between them. "And the best thing I did, the really big one, was convincing that woman to have an affair with you! Oh, boy, that was a really neat trick! You know why,

Bob? Because no woman in her right mind would ever let you fuck her. That took some doing, that little fling of yours that I arranged."

Helen watched Bob's hand go slack, the gun hanging loose at his side. Confusion creased his face, and he stared at Allison as if he'd never seen her before in his life. "You're out of your fucking mind, Al," he mumbled.

"That's right, Bob. I had to be insane to marry a shithead like you." Allison smiled a cold hard smile at him. "You think killing me will get something back for you? It'll get you a short walk to the gas chamber, or to a hypodermic full of poison, or whatever they're using for the death penalty these days. Go ahead and shoot. I don't give a fuck, as long as you burn in hell for it."

Now, Helen ordered herself. Bob never looked in her direction as she swung her right leg around in an arc that connected her foot with the legs of a kitchen chair. The chair flew across the room and slammed into his knees. He yelled out in surprise and pain, bent over and grabbed his knees. The gun fell to the floor with a thud, scattering glass in a nimbus with the impact. Helen rolled over, fearful that it might go off and ricochet into her, then kicked again. The gun spun around, then veered off beside the refrigerator. If Helen couldn't get to it, neither could Bob.

Allison had already run from the room. Helen saw the phone in her hand, then heard her voice as she spoke frantically to the police.

Bob, still clutching his knees, stumbled over toward Helen. She'd pulled herself up and heaved the table at him, lunging forward with all her weight in the push. Awkward from the blow to his legs, Bob didn't get out of the way in time. The edge of the table hit the same wrenched knee, and he screamed at Helen, "Fuck you, bulldyke!"

The effort to get the words out distracted him as she slithered around the table. With all the strength she had left, she shoved her fist into his belly, plunging deep into the slack flesh. His eyes widened as the wind was knocked out of him and she followed up with a sharp thrust of her knee to his groin.

After that, he was very quiet. Before he was able to get any more words out, Helen pulled the gun out from where it had gotten wedged between the cabinet and the refrigerator.

She was still standing there, Allison trembling behind her, when the police arrived. Helen and Allison waited, huddled together on the living room sofa, as one of the officers spoke with Bob in the kitchen.

"Will you be coming down to the station to press charges, Ms. Young?"

Allison didn't answer right away.

"Ms. Young," the officer repeated, his voice tired and exasperated, "will you —"

"No. No, I won't."

Helen stared at her in amazement. She was too stunned to speak.

Allison's face was a blank. The green eyes were set, dark and dull, and her mouth was grim. "No."

The officer shook his head. "Your choice, ma'am." He joined his partner, flipping his notebook shut as he walked. Helen heard chuckles coming from the kitchen, and soon both officers trooped out, with Bob taking up the rear. Helen saw no restraints, no concern on the part of the police at Bob's freedom.

"It'll just be a warning, a little talk and a slap on the hand," Helen said, watching through the front window as Bob stalked off into the fog and the black and white car drove off downtown. "Why, Allison?" she asked as gently as she could. "Why didn't you press charges?"

Allison looked up. Silent tears streamed down her cheeks. "If you only knew," she said, "how many times I've tried. How many lectures Bob has heard, how often I've had to listen to policemen and judges and lawyers and therapists laughing it off. It never does any good. They're all the same, they —"

"It's okay, it's okay." Helen hugged her, rocking her as she wept. How could she presume to dictate Allison's behavior? What right did she have?

"You think I'm weak and terrible, don't you?"

Helen leaned back to look into Allison's face. "I would never think that. Never. You've dealt with more pain in the past few years than I have in a lifetime. I'm just worried about you. I want you to be safe." Helen stopped herself before she blurted out something she'd regret.

Allison's sobs abated, and she dried her eyes. "I sure know how to give a girl a good time, don't I?"

Helen mustered up a smile. "I wouldn't have traded it for the world."

Allison smiled back, wryly, unbelieving. "I think I'd better get home. Are you going back to Lafayette?"

Helen nodded, taken aback at the sudden chill in

her voice. She watched Allison go off into the bedroom and emerge fully dressed.

"I think I'll go see the real estate agent today," Allison said. "See if those people are really interested in the house."

"Sure. I'll drop you off."

Allison stopped at the door. "Helen, thank you. I don't have any idea what I should say to you. I mean, last night — then this morning —"

"Hush." Helen touched Allison's lips with her fingers. "You don't have to say anything or do anything. Let's just get you home."

"I ?— I'm almost afraid to ask you, but later today —"

"Here's my number." Helen dug a card out of her pocket, paused to scratch her home phone number under the office number. "Call me later, when you're ready."

"Who said you could be so sweet and understanding? Damnit, I hate it when that happens," Allison said as they got in the car and headed back to Lafayette.

Chapter Twelve

"So, Helen! Tell me all about her."

Helen looked up from her sandwich — they made a great turkey and cheese on focaccia — and smiled at Ramona. Java Jones was not very busy today. Usually the place was packed during the stretch between eleven-thirty and two p.m. The sunshine, which had tempted people out of doors and into the streets of Lafayette yesterday morning, was gone as if never to return, lurking somewhere in the fog.

"Wish there was something to tell, Ramona." Helen took another bite of her sandwich and surveyed the quiet café. "Still having that open house on Saturday?"

"Halloween, from noon until closing. Will you be here?"

"As long as you don't make me wear a costume." Paper pumpkins and crepe witches festooned the counters, and cartoon ghosts had been painted on the windows. Some wit had painted lavender and rainbow scarves around the necks of the smiling spirits.

"Well, I was thinking I might come as a straight woman. What do you think?"

Helen smiled again. "That I'd have to see. I wonder if Frieda will be there."

Ramona shrugged and stood up. "Hard to say, with Jill being in trouble. Maybe they won't show."

Helen shook her head. "All right, Ramona, quit showing off! I know you have your finger on the pulse of the town, you don't have to prove it to me."

"Well, in these days of non-alcoholic beverages, the café owner, like the therapist and the hairstylist, is a fount of information." Ramona retied her apron and went back into the kitchen while Helen finished her sandwich.

It was almost one o'clock, and the sun was still hiding. Helen decided to give herself a morning off from holding a picket sign, especially since she was sure that there'd be a heavy police presence there. She made a mental note to deduct this morning's hours from her final invoice to the Linville when it was time for payment.

She'd driven by the clinic via the frontage road. Slowing down to see the site where Melinda's body was found, Helen was surprised at the sight of a black Jaguar blocking the turnoff. Inside, two figures were gesturing and pointing down the road toward the freeway. Strange — people were apparently still morbidly fascinated at the idea of murder. Helen watched as the car pulled forward slowly, then did a three-point turn to get back out on the main street. The Jag whirred by her own humbler vehicle. Curious, Helen followed them right into the parking lot of Java Jones. At least her surveillance could include a decent lunch. She tucked her file on the Linville case under her arm and went inside to greet Ramona.

Now, one sandwich later, at the thought of wrapping up her investigation, Helen grimaced at the notepad she'd been jotting on for the past half-hour. After taking a much-subdued Allison home without knowing if she'd ever hear from her again, Helen thought she'd drown her sorrows in a good lunch and work up some notes on the case. So far, all she had was lots of practice at sign-holding, a few sore muscles and a firm belief that the vandals were not disguised as conservative Christian demonstrators. In fact, given the rather juvenile nature of the vandalism so far, Helen was more inclined to think about a bunch of kids like Cam and his cohorts. It would make sense, she reasoned. Maybe a way to get attention from his aging and fanatical parents? As well as throw a monkey wrench into their life's work? Maybe.

She sighed and leaned back in the chair, careful not to stretch too hard. Her back still hurt from being hurled onto her kitchen floor this morning. Once again she marveled at the variety of people Java Jones attracted.

For example, tucked away at one of the small

glass-topped tables near the entrance, two grandmotherly patrons sipped at tall coffee drinks topped with whipped cream, carefully holding their strings of pearls so as not to dip them in the rich dark liquid. Judging by the scent that had wafted in with them, they'd probably just emerged from under a hairdryer at the salon next door where they had their hair blued every week.

The café was a popular meeting place for such ladies. Once Helen had heard two of them chattering about the rainbow sign in the window. "Isn't it pretty? I wonder where I can get one!" one had gushed. At the time Helen had refrained from suggesting that she visit Castro Street in San Francisco.

Behind her, at the longest table in the room, six men were gathered over roast beef to conduct some kind of luncheon sales meeting. Between laptops and computer reports and small-scale flip charts, these men chomped down on Ramona's cooking. Helen had been informed that this was a regular twice-weekly meeting at the café.

The only people she couldn't place were the two men seated at the coffee bar, where Ramona, when she was cooking, presided over the hissing espresso machine. Both men were talking on cell phones in angry whispers. Their suits looked expensive, even for Lafayette, and it was their Jaguar parked outside.

Ramona stopped by to refill Helen's coffee cup. "Am I being investigated?" she asked.

"Ramona, your life is an open book. To know you is to love you. Actually, I wanted to pick your brain. Who are those two?"

Ramona looked toward the counter, then turned

back to Helen, rolling her eyes. "Real big spenders. They've been here every day for a week now, and they never eat. Just coffee, coffee, coffee." She took her time clearing away the remains of Helen's lunch. "Rumor has it," she said in a voice perfectly pitched not to reach beyond Helen's table, "that they're developers looking for a place to put up the mall."

"What mall?"

"I forget, you city folks don't think anything goes on in the sticks." She took out a clean cloth and wiped the glass table as she spoke. "All the business owners in Lafayette are about ready to tear their hair out. The city council has been inviting guys like these two in to check out what few blades of grass we still got left so they can build some God-awful mall. You know, fast-food and glitzy boutiques and costume jewelry priced like the Hope Diamond." Ramona shook her head. "When I opened up this place three years ago — you remember, Helen, you were there — I wanted it because it was a quiet little homey town. Lots of mom and pop operations. That'll be a thing of the past if this mall deal goes through."

Although Helen thought she knew the answer, she asked, "Where are they thinking of putting the mall? It's not like there's a lot of land just sitting around empty."

Ramona tucked the cloth back into her apron. "Right in back of the Linville. Same place they found that woman two days ago."

Unable to neglect her patrons any longer, Ramona moved away, listening to a variety of requests as she headed back for the kitchen. Helen saw one of the men at the counter toss a few bills between the half-empty cups and pocket his phone. Both men left without a glance at Helen.

As soon as they'd climbed into the Jaguar, Helen dug money from her pockets, left it on the table with a quick wave to Ramona, then hurried to her own car. She followed the Jag until it zipped up to the freeway, weaving between other cars and disappearing in the afternoon commute.

"Fuck," she muttered. After a moment's thought she turned back and drove to the frontage road. So what was the big attraction about this particular site?

Of course, it had to be the rapid transit system. Shoppers from all over the Bay Area could hop on a train and shuttle to this spot with ease. And there would be plenty of consumers who'd insist on driving and parking — so there would have to be a parking lot or parking building, with fees and tickets and lots of revenue for those smart enough and quick enough to get in on the project early.

Helen pulled over — she was just at the spot where Melinda's car had been found, and yellow crime-scene tape still flapped from a couple of nearby trees — and got out of her car. Yes, she could see why developers would be very interested. They'd probably even work the little creek into the design, somehow. Maybe put in a sort of romantic bridge for lovers to tryst on.

"Well. Not in my back yard." Helen laughed at herself when she realized she sounded just like all the Lafayette citizens who objected to having the Linville in their town. As she walked back to her car a sliver of the ragged yellow tape blew across the road. She followed it with her eyes until it landed soundlessly on the soggy sneaker sticking out of the creek.

Helen slammed the car door shut again and went slowly toward the water. The stream was spilling and gurgling loudly over rocks and grasses, bursting from the rain. Anything in the water, placed at an angle like that, would be driven along by the steady current, not stationary in all that swirling motion. Why the hell would a shoe stick up that way?

And then she saw the swollen, discolored face of Cam Logan. One leg had been twisted up in the razor-edged weeds that were tangled enough, apparently, to keep the corpse in place in spite of the bulging current. The wisp of yellow tape caught on the toe of his shoe, then lifted in a gust of cold air to settle on the stream's surface and spin off into oblivion.

Helen's training kept her calm and observant. She knelt down in the mud and looked hard. Cam was wearing the same baggy clothes she'd seen on him yesterday. An ugly dent in his forehead, outlined with livid purple blotches, made her hope he'd been unconscious or already dead when held under the water. She was no coroner, but she'd also seen her share of drowning victims and recognized the bloating and the weird distortion that that kind of death could cause.

She resisted the urge to reach under the water and close his right eyelid which for some reason had opened. The dead boy seemed to be winking at her ghoulishly and she looked away quickly to check out the rest of the scene.

On the other bank of the stream, almost close

enough to reach and grab, was a full garbage bag, the big industrial size often used for yard and lawn work. She didn't dare cross the stream and disturb anything, but poking out of the bag Helen saw a nozzle — the kind found on cans of spray paint. She bet the bag also contained kerosene and rags and odds and ends similar to things found at the Linville vandalism sites.

Now was not the time to speculate on the cause of Cam's death. She got up and headed for her car and her cell phone, then suddenly turned back. Crouching down again, she peered into the murky water near the boy's head.

It bobbed and bounced in the stream, the tongue lolling along his bloated cheeks. The eye that refused to shut seemed to glare at her as she leaned in close.

Yes, it was there. The gun, just heavy enough to resist the tug of the current, lay on a bed of smooth pebbles next to Cam's shoulder. Had it been there all along, since Melinda's murder, or had it only recently landed in the stream?

With a sense of desperate urgency Helen slipped her way back up to her car. "Fuck!" she shouted out into the emptiness of the frontage road. The cell phone was right where Allison had left it this morning, on the counter in the kitchen. She'd have to drive somewhere, since she couldn't exactly go into the clinic past the protesters. Helen remembered seeing a gas station at the end of the road, under the overpass of the freeway.

And she'd better hurry, because there was no telling how much longer Cam's body would stay in that position. Under normal circumstances, the stream was probably nothing more than a faint trickle of moisture, barely enough for wild ducks to swim in. Right now, though, it was flowing with impressive force. In fact, there was no way of knowing yet if indeed that's where he died. He might have been struck and dumped into the water at any point along the frontage road, his body pushed and pulled by the stream to its present position.

Even more reason to hurry, Helen thought. At the gas station, a middle-aged attendant, grimed and smudged with grease, trotted out to meet her. Helen ignored him and ran to the pay phone.

She was put on hold for the space of a few seconds while someone went to fetch someone else. While waiting, she kept her eyes on the frontage road directly ahead.

"Yes, I'm still here. This is an emergency —"

She was cut off again. Great. Exasperated, still aching from her busy morning, Helen leaned her head against the cool glass of the phone booth. Lord knows she was tired, so maybe she imagined that small dark figure running down the road, almost a mile away. She peered through the glass. Nothing. Was she that tired?

"Lieutenant Macabee, can I help you?"

"Yes, sir, you can."

Chapter Thirteen

At least the wind had died down, Helen thought. In cold, still air the two men in plain blue overalls struggled to load Cam's body onto a stretcher. She looked away as one of the men slipped in the mud, cursed, and grabbed the corpse to keep it from slipping out from under the restraints and back into the water. One of the men must have made some blackly humorous comment, because a wave of laughter burst out from the collected crime scene workers huddled near the water's edge.

Unbidden, morgue scenes, engraved on Helen's

memory from her years working homicide in Berkeley, started parading through her mind. She knew exactly what the Logans would face — the walk through the halls of the morgue in Martinez, the county seat, the twinges of nausea at the biting scent of a dozen chemicals that never quite hid the odor of death, the awful moments of hope and terror before the curtain was drawn back and the body of their son revealed to them. Did the staff at Martinez have a nickname for their work environment, borne of desperate laughter as they coped with the flood of death? "Got to go to the Fridge," they used to say with wry smiles, and off they'd go to witness an autopsy or talk to a pathologist.

The wagon carrying Cam's remains squelched off through the mud. Helen felt a rush of relief. It had never failed — once the body was gone, a great deal of tension was gone, too. Now it would be easier to maintain a professional demeanor, to focus on the scene itself.

Damn, but it was cold. How much longer would she have to be there, answering questions and putting up with the looks and the whispers all around her? Of course, these guys were just doing their job. And it was possible she'd remember some small detail, anything that would send them after Cam's killer. She knew the drill. She'd told them everything, including reiterating her involvement with the Logans and their followers, just as she'd done before, when Melinda's body had been found.

"Will you be heading back to Berkeley, Ms. Black?"

The voice rasping behind her startled Helen. She

turned to find Lieutenant Macabee standing a few feet behind her, his big flat feet planted firmly on the asphalt of the frontage road.

She forced a smile. "Probably. I don't see any reason to stay," and a sadness about Allison rose up in her, but she couldn't linger in Lafayette, hoping for a chance to talk to the woman. "Unless you'd like me to."

"Not necessary." He looked nothing like the image Helen had formed while talking to him on the telephone. The voice, rich and deep and sensual, had formed in her thoughts as a tall, dark and handsome stranger.

Macabee moved quickly for such a big man. Silently, too. He had big freckled paws, stuffed into tight leather gloves, and he twined his fingers together as he and Helen stood watching the wagon pull away. His moon-face, freckled and topped with incredibly curly pale red hair, swiveled and followed the vehicle as it rolled, lights flashing but no sirens wailing — no need — across the bumps and pits of the road and on to the freeway.

"Sorry I couldn't talk to you before," he said, turning his bulk to face her. Helen stared, disconcerted — his eyes were an indeterminate color, sort of a muddy grayish brown.

"No problem," she finally responded. "You had a lot to do. I remember what it's like."

Her attempt at camaraderie was clearly a mistake. His face folded in distaste. "Yes, your — ah — reputation has preceded you. How long has it been now, since you left police work?"

"Six years." Helen watched as he removed one

glove, his eyes fixed on the small depression in the mud left by Cam's body. "You don't ever forget it, though."

"No, I expect you don't." The glove slid back on and he faced her again. "My boys tell me you informed them a couple of days ago that you're on a case out here."

"Yes." Helen offered nothing else, waiting to see what he would say next. At the time, the officer questioning her at the scene of Melinda's death, just about twenty yards from the place Macabee now stood, had been disbelieving when she revealed her identity. When her story had checked out she'd expected to talk to the lieutenant in charge, but after a few more questions they'd let her go. She'd assumed they'd at least want to talk to her about her investigation, but to her surprise there'd been no further comment.

"As I said, your reputation came before you did." Macabee began to stroll toward his car, forcing Helen to follow him. "You made quite a name for yourself in Berkeley."

Helen steeled herself. She knew what was coming next. "I'm flattered you took the time to check me out," she said in neutral tones. "Of course, what you heard depends on who you talked to."

"That's irrelevant. What I heard was enough to make me realize I should have been informed of your presence here two days ago." He stopped, pulled a cigar from some inner pocket and dug for a lighter in another pocket. Helen watched as he puffed smoke into the air over the place where Cam had recently died. "Naturally, I don't have to tell you to keep quiet about whatever you think you saw here. And to stick around the area until this is wrapped up."

Helen sighed. She turned away from Macabee, staring out across the weeds and grasses to the BART rails. A train pulled in from the west — from San Francisco — and a handful of people scurried out to stairways and escalators, eager to get out of the cold. Once again Helen had to face the mixture of homophobia and misogyny she'd fought all her life. It was clear to her, from the way Macabee could barely bring himself to meet her eyes, that he felt only disgust at the idea of a woman detective who, to top it off, was experienced in homicide investigations.

"Just stay out of my way, and keep your mouth shut," he was saying, "and we'll —"

"Hey, Mac!"

"Yeah?" He grabbed the phone carried over by some hapless assistant, barked into it for a moment, then tossed it back to the officer. "I have to get moving," he said to Helen, edging his bulk past her to his car. "The Logans are on their way to the locker."

"The —" Of course. The Fridge.

"I'll have to get moving to be there to meet them." His door slammed shut and his moon face loomed out at her. "Remember what I said. I don't want to have to repeat it. I hate saying things twice."

In a puff of cigar smoke and a spout of exhaust Macabee whipped his car around and sped off. Helen walked slowly back toward her car, hoping her anger would dissipate quickly. As it was, an entire day had been taken up with equal amounts of terror and frustration. The sun was finally breaking through the fog as the afternoon drew to a close. A few rays winked across the stream at her and she watched as the orange and gold sphere curved over the ridge of the train station.

Just when she'd made it to her car and opened the door she heard the cries of excitement coming from the other side of the stream bed. A gang of uniformed officers rushed to the site where the shouting had originated. Helen paused, wondering what they'd found. Apparently it was enough to get them all worked up, because one man sloshed back through the creek and raced for his car. She heard the squawk of the radio as he communicated with the dispatcher.

Damn. Probably not a good idea to hang around right now. Helen had almost gotten into her car when something moved at the edge of her peripheral vision. Was it — yes, the small dark figure she thought she'd seen hours ago, huddled down low in the weeds. It was getting too dark to make out any features. Helen decided to wait near her car for a few minutes.

She was glad she did, because as the shadow in the grass inched closer to where the police were working, Helen was able to creep up and get a look at whatever had caused all the commotion. The last few shreds of sunlight picked up reflections off the cans of red spray paint as they spilled out of the thick, industrial-size garbage bag. Helen was stunned. How could they have missed it before? It must have made a very recent appearance on the scene — possibly just the night before, when she guessed Cam had died. Pieces of the puzzle clicked and spun in

Helen's mind as she stood quietly, watching the tableau of discovery playing out by the creek.

Somewhere along here the vandals had kept their equipment, close to the scene of their activities. Perhaps they'd moved their stuff around, never staying in the same place twice. Where would they have been the night of Melinda's murder? Someplace sheltered, she was certain, to keep out of the rain and wind. As these thoughts roved through her mind, Helen looked around her. Was there any kind of structure nearby? No, that wouldn't work. It would have been searched as soon as Melinda's body was found. Well, some sort of natural opening or cave or something near the water?

Her gaze following the line of the stream, Helen was once again distracted by the arrival of a BART train. The answer was right there, under the long silver line of the train that sped smoothly into the station. Of course. The concrete supports of the rails that were suspended high over the town would provide several useful niches for one or two plastic bags concealed during the night. And the stations closed down after midnight — perfect timing. Cam — Helen was convinced he'd been the vandals' ringleader — would have been here last night. Had he been hiding in the grass the night of Melinda's death, too? What kind of connection did he have to all this? And then there was the gun. The puzzle pieces swirled around in her thoughts, too many rushing too fast for her to make sense of them.

Helen had moved as close as she dared to the stream, and the light was fading fast. She needed to go home, collect her thoughts, feed her cat, try to find something to eat. Helen glanced to her left. The shadow was moving, slithering away through the tangle of weeds. Unable to break away, Helen watched as it made a wide swath in the muddy expanse of the field towards the BART station.

When the figure made it past the police and started to run in the direction of the trains, Helen raced for her car and sped off in search of a way to the station. If she was right, there was a turnoff from the frontage road — to hell with the "one way" arrow pointing at her. She flew along the wet pavement, fortunately unopposed. She looked left, locating and fixing the position of the shadow as it sped on some hidden path and reached the ement below the rails spanning overhead.

Traffic was heading out and away from the station as commuters, busy with briefcases and bags, loaded up cars and took off for home. Helen easily found a parking space near the entrance. At least she didn't have to worry about a parking ticket, since it was already after six and parking was free in train lots once rush hours were over. Now the only problem, she reminded herself, was to catch up with shadow and —

A ticket. "Shit." She muttered curses and fished for change. Any amount over eighty cents would get her into the system. She'd just have to add on ticket value before exiting at one of the many machines scattered around each station. Yes, thank God, a whole dollar in quarters. Forcing herself to be calm Helen shoved the coins into a ticket machine after waiting behind two elderly women who took at least twelve hours to complete their transactions and totter off into the station.

She'd just heard the whir and click of the ticket

machine and grabbed her blue and white ticket from the slot when the shadow caught her eye again. Gabriella Espinoza locked stares with her. Tonight, clad in the usual baggy clothes, she looked very young and very scared. Her jeans were coated with mud still wet and gleaming under the harsh lights of the station.

As quickly as if Helen had imagined her, Gabi vanished through the turnstile and disappeared. Helen raced after her, bumping and nudging tired commuters out of her way, ignoring the curses shouted at her from behind.

A pair of muddy sneakers pounded the stairs to her right. Gabi was heading toward San Francisco. Helen ran after her — Jesus, she was out of shape — as she heard the throb of an approaching train.

"San Francisco train arriving at Lafayette station," the agent announced over the usually unintelligible PA system. Helen heard the beep of opening doors, and then had to fight her way through a thicket of people coursing quickly down the stairs she was trying to climb. "Fuck," she said with a grunt as she pushed her way past outraged patrons. She had to make this train.

Just as the doors beeped again and slid shut Helen landed safely in the car. Damn, it was full of people and stifling. She stood to catch her breath, trying not to lean on the people jammed in around her, aware that her heavy gasps for air and flushed face garnered some attention. Not much, though — people who frequented the BART system were used to seeing just about everything, from exhausted travelers to crazed street people to fights to parties to musicians to whatever.

Now she had to offend others yet again in her search through the cars. Gabi must have seen her standing there, talking to Macabee while the police examined the crime scene, Helen thought as she eased her way through knots of people trying to read newspapers and hold on at the same time as the train lurched westward. How deeply had the girl been involved in the vandalism? Or the murder of Melinda Wright, for that matter?

After tussling her way through three cars, Helen spotted her. She was wedged near the doors to Helen's left, between a pregnant woman pale with exhaustion and two men in expensive suits arguing about some recent football game. The girl constantly looked around the car, watching for Helen. When their eyes met, Gabi froze with fear. She tried to break out of the spot she was in, but Helen was quicker. Helen was almost within reach of Gabi when the train pulled into the station.

A muffled beep of the train's horn announced their arrival. "MacArthur Station," the driver intoned. "Arriving at MacArthur Station, first transfer point in the BART system for the Concord, Fremont and Richmond lines."

The doors immediately behind Gabi slid open, and she disappeared. Helen fought her way off the train. At least she could breathe again, and she inhaled big gulps of fresh air. There she was — running off to the central staircase. As Helen flew down the steps she heard the rumble of another arriving train overhead. Helen prayed that Gabi wouldn't scurry into another train that would take her to Richmond, or Fremont — she didn't think she'd be able to move fast enough through the crowds to reach the train before the doors slid shut and the cars moved away.

She heaved a sigh of relief as Gabi reappeared, her slim body moving through the exiting turnstile and standing, breathless, on the wide expanse of the station entrance. It was completely dark now. Helen piled coins in her palm, shoved her ticket in the add-fare machine, and thrust money in without bothering to count how much she had or how much she needed. She kept it up until a fresh ticket spat out at her, then frantically nudged people aside to get through the turnstile.

Gabi was walking away fast, frequently turning to look behind her. As soon as she saw Helen she broke once again into a run, loping easily toward Telegraph Avenue, one of the arteries connecting Oakland to Berkeley. Helen rolled her eyes. She'd really meant to take up running again, soon, she told herself as she forced her body to move. Of course, her activities this morning hadn't been much help, she reminded herself, thinking of the confrontation with Bob in her kitchen. "It's a jam-packed, fun-filled lifestyle," she muttered as she reached the corner of Telegraph and 51st Street.

Gabi was only just out of reach, and Helen strained to close the final few yards that separated them. With aching arms and chest, Helen grabbed her sweatshirt with just enough strength to stop her from running.

"That's it, kid," Helen gasped, using her other hand to wipe sweat from her face. "End of the line," she managed to get out.

Gabi turned a pale terrified face to Helen. "Please," she whispered. "Please don't tell them, I — please —"

"Sorry, kid. You and I have a bone to pick."

Chapter Fourteen

Carmen's apartment was located on 41st Street, near Telegraph and the BART station where Helen had finally caught up with Gabi. The building was old but beautifully designed, with spacious windows and an enclosed courtyard. True — iron grills barred all the front floor windows, and a massive security gate distracted the passersby from noticing the flower beds, but this was not a section of Oakland that encouraged open windows and unlocked doors.

When Gabi had timidly knocked on her sister's door, after Helen had used all her persuasive powers on the girl, Carmen had at first refused to let her in. It was only when Helen moved so that Carmen could see her face in the hallway that Carmen had opened the door. The place was almost completely dark — the only light in the room came from an aging television set, so outdated that it sported rabbit-ear antennae. The place, though furnished with shabby second-hand pieces, was spotless. All the blinds were closed tight.

"What have you done now, Gabi?"

"Nothing. I — please let us in. Helen is here."

"Yes, I can see that. What the hell you doing bringing a private eye to my house? You know what's gonna happen to *abuela* and *abuelo* because you're such a stupid kid? Huh?"

"It's not her fault, Carmen. I followed her here." Helen strode into the room before Carmen could shut her out.

Carmen glared at her sister but brought her a cold soda as well as offering one to Helen. "This stupid kid, I told her not to come to this place until I figured out what I'm gonna do," she muttered, sliding onto the arm of the chair where Gabi sat, forlorn and tearstained. "I told my mother, too — don't come near here. I'm not going to be home for a few days, while I get all this shit sorted out." Carmen pretended to smack her sister on the head, but the threatened blow turned into a caress. "*Mija,* you gonna cause me such grief."

Helen watched them, forcing herself to keep from eyeing the television set over to her right. Carmen had turned the volume completely down, but Helen couldn't help sneaking a glance now and then to see if the news had come on with any stories about Cam Logan.

"I think everyone at the clinic is wondering if you're okay. Maybe you should give them a call, Carmen."

"Bullshit! That bitch, Melinda Wright — I'm glad she's dead. I hated her. She was gonna call the —"

"Carmen, no!" Gabi pulled her sister's sleeve, nearly knocking her down to the floor with the urgent gesture. "This bitch that followed me here, she's going to go right to the cops. She'll tell them everything."

"So what? You think they don't already know something about us?"

"Look," Helen interrupted, "I didn't come here to turn anyone in to the police for anything. I don't even know what the hell you're talking about." Frustrated and torn between listening to the sisters fight or watching television news, Helen got up and went to the TV set to turn it off. "All I know is that you, Gabi, were hanging out at the place where Cam Logan died. You were watching the police, and you were watching me. I think you'd better start talking. You too, Carmen."

Gabi started to cry again. "Your sister saw something terrible today," Helen began.

"What? Her report card?"

Helen allowed a smile at that one. "No, Carmen, I'm afraid not," and she went on to describe what she herself had seen on the frontage road that afternoon.

Carmen's eyes glazed over and she stared hard at Helen, her gaze never straying to light on Gabi, but her hand stroking Gabi's long hair as she listened. When Helen was finished, Carmen got up from the chair and walked into the kitchen. Helen heard her punching in numbers on a telephone, then there was a conversation in Spanish that was too quick and too whispered for her to decipher.

"She's talking to Mama," Gabi said, wiping her nose with the sleeve of her sweatshirt. "I'm gonna get killed when I get home."

"Oh, I doubt it. I might kill you first. I'm getting too old to be chasing nice young girls on BART trains."

Gabi smiled briefly, just a glimmer across her face, then her features folded over in sadness. "Everyone says I'm not a nice young girl. Not with the kids I hang with."

"And she's not." Carmen came back from the kitchen, this time seating herself on the sofa next to Helen. "Papa is on his way over, *mija*. He'll be here in about half an hour. They're not angry, they just want you home safe."

"Carmen, I'm sorry! I don't want anyone to get into trouble!"

A fresh wave of tears followed, and Helen let them have a few moments of emotional reunion. "I know you've had a rough few days. I'm not going to intrude on you much longer, but I really need some answers," she finally said as gently as she could. "And I'm sure we'd all prefer to talk about this before your father gets here."

"Come on." Carmen nudged Gabi with her elbow. "Tell her what you told me."

Gabi's story was close to what Helen had suspected. When the school year started, Gabi's born-again parents had decided to place her in Dr. Logan's Christian High School in Lafayette. "They figured it would be a safe place for me, so I wouldn't hang out with the wrong kids," Gabi said, rolling her eyes in exasperation at the dim wits of her parents. And so it had been — until she'd met Cam Logan. "I mean, I thought it was so cool, him being Dr. Logan's son, and acting like he liked me and everything," Gabi continued, her voice trembling with the memory. "I was going to be popular, you know? It was great, 'cause I'm almost the only Chicana there at the school. I didn't think none of those whites would like me or nothing."

Everything had been fine, she said, until the night of the first football game, in mid-September. Logan High was facing off another Christian school, the Avengers from Alameda. Gabi recalled the decorations and pep rallies and excited plans. It was all going to be so much fun, when all her new friends went to the game and went out afterwards.

That was when Cam got his idea. "I think he just wanted to get to his old man or something — you know, get him in trouble or make him upset. Anyway, he got it all worked out and kept hinting to us about the great stuff he was gonna do that Friday night."

Gabi had shown up at the school grounds, ready to have a good time. "We all got in Cam's car — he had his old man's station wagon — and then we were headed the wrong way. Everyone started to yell at him, 'Hey look, stupid, you're supposed to turn here, the football field is that way,' shit like that." But Cam had driven on, following his own route. Gabi remembered sitting in the front seat next to him, watching that hawk nose and weak chin, thinking how like his father he looked in the dark. "I knew right away where we was going — I mean, I been to the Linville enough times to meet Carmen, right? So here I am, yelling out, 'Hey, Cam, that's the clinic, and what are we doing here?'" Gabi had been unfamiliar with the frontage road, but Cam drove through the total darkness there as if he'd been there many times before. Everyone else in the car was silent, fearful, not sure what was happening. Cam had told them exactly what to do. "There was this big garbage bag, you know, like the ones the police had today. He'd put all kinds of shit into it, like paint and gasoline in those square cans, old towels and stuff. He told us all what to do."

"And you did it."

Gabi nodded. Another tear spilled down her cheeks but she choked back sobs and went on. "I swear, I never did nothing to that place. All I did was stand and watch. Cam, he told me to keep my eyes on the road in case anybody came along. Then he took us to this place in the fence and we climbed through it." Gabi shuddered. Her eyes stared wide and dark into nothingness, and Helen knew she was reliving the night it all began, seeing things no one else could see. "I was so scared! I didn't know what to do if somebody came. I just knew we was all going to be in really bad shit if we got caught."

"But you didn't get caught. How many other times, Gabi?"

"Just that one time, I swear! Cam — he tried to get me to go more, but I wouldn't do it. He —" Gabi glanced over at her sister, who nodded for her to go on. "Cam kissed me and told me he'd never seen any girl so beautiful. I didn't really believe him, 'cause I know guys talk a lot of shit just to screw girls, but I hoped — I hoped I could be friends, hang with his friends, you know, that kind of shit."

"How long were you there, Gabi?"

She shrugged, and her words came out tired and drained of feeling. "I don't know. Not long. Maybe not even an hour. After they sprayed the place and set fire to some stuff, the guys all got in the car. Cam drove us over by the BART station, you know, to that concrete thing with the holes in it?"

Helen nodded — one of the concrete supports holding up the monorail, carved with decorative niches. Jammed in just right, the garbage bag would be unnoticed, and Cam would have moved it frequently, going from niche to niche.

"He told us to say we were at the football game, that no one would care enough to ask us questions." Gabi had finished now, Helen saw. Exhausted by the events of the day, heavy lids drooped over her eyes.

Helen rushed a few more questions at her. "Why were you there today, Gabi?"

"I was worried when Cam didn't make it to school. I thought he might be putting more stuff out there, paint and stuff. And the gun scared me."

"That was what he showed you in the cemetery that day, wasn't it?"

Gabi stopped in mid-yawn. "You knew about that? But no one else was there! How did you know?"

"Was it the gun?"

"Yeah." She continued to stare at Helen as if she'd just performed an amazing magic trick. "He wouldn't tell us nothing about how he got it, where it came from. The other kids were too afraid to look for him, but I needed to find out. I thought — well, I know that lady, who was at the clinic —"

"Melinda Wright," spat out Carmen, as if she'd tasted something incredibly foul.

"Yeah, the one who got killed. I knew she was shot in the head, and I knew Cam had a gun from somewhere."

"So what do you think, Gabi? Did Cam kill her?"

She seemed taken aback by the question. "Then why did he get killed, if he's the one who had the gun all along? Besides, Cam wasn't like that."

"Wasn't like what? According to you, he was perfectly capable of arson and vandalism and damaging property."

"No, no, you don't get it." She glanced at Carmen, who shrugged and turned a confused look to Helen. "He was such a weasel, a — a coward. Yeah, that's it. He'd only do what was safe to do. I mean, in the dark, with no one around. Not even his old man. He was too scared of him to do anything to his face." Gabi shook her head vigorously and folded her arms, certain she was right. "Cam would never kill nobody."

Helen tried a few more questions, but Gabi was clearly at the end of her energy. Soon a piercing buzz announced that the girls' father waited outside.

Gabi seemed to get a second wind when she heard Papa's voice. "I'll go, Carmen," she protested when her sister got up to let him in. "I just want to go home now, okay?" For a moment Helen saw the little girl under the jaded demeanor and torn jeans.

"All right, kid. Tell Papa I'll see him on Saturday."

When the door had slammed behind Gabi, Helen smiled at Carmen. "Now it's your turn. You've got a lot of people wondering where you've been."

Carmen stood at the door, her back to Helen. "I don't mean for anyone to get worried, you know? It's just — I think I scared myself when that Wright bitch got killed." Carmen sighed and crossed the room to flop on the sofa, stopping long enough to switch on a lamp. For the first time Helen saw the heavy dark circles under her eyes, the strain that wasn't covered with perfect makeup. "It's my grandparents. They've been in California since long before I was born, but —" She stopped, staring at Helen, considering something.

"Carmen, anything you say here — well, you'll just have to trust me. Unless it has something to do with my investigation, or with the murders of Melinda Wright and Cam Logan, I'm not about to repeat a word you tell me tonight."

Carmen closed her eyes, screwing them tight shut and rubbing her hands over her face. "I don't know if I can trust you, but the good lord knows I'm so tired of all this I can't stand it. My grandparents are not here legally. No papers. No green card. No nothing. It was all a lie. They paid this lawyer a lot of money to get them their papers fixed, a long, long time ago."

"But, I don't get it, Carmen. What does that have to do with Melinda Wright's death? Why would you run away?"

"That bitch from hell was watching me. Ever since that proposition got passed a couple years ago — you know, the one about illegal immigration — I been so scared they gonna get my *abuelito* and *abuelita* and take them away. They're old, Helen. They can't handle it."

Yes, Helen remembered — remembered her own shock and amazement when the state of California, long regarded as a bastion of liberal thought and tolerance, had voted in favor of legislation that would severely punish not just illegal aliens, but their children. Denial of medical care and education, immediate deportation and continual harassment were only a few of the choice options now potentially open to a variety of regulatory bodies. Helen had sat in complete astonishment when the voting results were in, at first refusing to believe the numbers.

"I already know what you gonna say — that no one would kick two sweet little old people out of the country, right? Hah!" Carmen snorted in disgust. "My dad, even my poor old dad who would never hurt anybody and has worked hard all his life and became a citizen, even — you know how many times some cop pulled him over just because he's Mexican?" Carmen shook her head, anger making her body rigid. "No, that bitch had it in for me. Going around making remarks about my accent — 'I can't understand you, Miss Espinoza, can't you talk more clearly?' And sometimes she'd get mad if I talked in Spanish to someone in the clinic. You know, lots of people coming in don't speak so good English. But the worst one — oh, the worst of all was when she asked me if any of my relatives could clean her house cheap."

Helen blinked in surprise. "You mean, she actually said that to you?"

"I swear before God, Helen." Carmen raised her right hand in mock salutation. "I wouldn't make anything like that up."

"You had every right to be furious at her, Carmen," Helen said quietly. "I think if you had said something to Dolores, she might have made sure that Melinda left the clinic."

"Oh, are you kidding? That poor stupid woman?" Carmen laughed again. "I'm sorry, but Dolores is crazy. She's so scared, like the rest of us, about losing her job, she's never gonna shake the boat and say something about anything."

Helen smiled at the spin Carmen had given the old adage, then said, "Why was Dolores so afraid of Melinda? And the rest of you. What was Melinda doing to that place?"

"Well, I guess it's not so much the bitch as Dave. I mean, Melinda was gonna get us shut down. Looking at our budget, making reports all the time, watching this and that. Those guys, the Trustees — they were gonna talk to her about what she saw there. They could do that, you know — shut us right down, just like that, if they weren't happy with how things were going."

Helen sat chewing on this information until Carmen tapped her on the arm.

"Hey, you okay in there? You got so quiet!"

When she stood up Helen realized how late it was. "God, I'm sorry, Carmen. I didn't notice the time." She gathered up her coat and hurried for the door. "I really want to thank you for talking to me.

151

And don't worry. It's entirely up to you whether or not you go back to the Linville. I promise not to say a word."

"Yeah, okay." From Carmen's expression Helen knew that she didn't believe her. But there was nothing Helen could do about that. The only thing that would teach Carmen to trust her was time.

Time. Shit, it was after eleven. Helen yawned as she drove back from Lafayette toward Berkeley. As she passed Shattuck Avenue, where her office was located in a rather expensive new building, Helen remembered that there was a phone number there — one that Carmen could use. Helen had never had cause to go to El Centro, the local Latino cultural organization. She'd kept the card of a woman who worked there, though, after talking with her at a dinner party. It was still in her desk, Helen was sure. Maybe someone at El Centro could talk to Carmen about her grandparents, either just to answer questions or to give legal advice.

Why not? Helen thought. It was on the way home. And maybe there'd actually be a payment in the mail instead of a bill.

The parking garage under the building, brightly lit and watched over by a tall, skinny woman who clearly enjoyed her uniform, was almost empty. Helen waved at Betty, who doffed her cap in greeting as Helen headed for the staircase.

Her office smelled musty. Helen hadn't been in it for several days, and it needed an airing. She cracked open a window that overlooked a cold silent street less than a mile from the university campus. Cold air rushed in as Helen noticed the red light blinking on her answering machine.

Her heart stopped when she heard Allison's voice. "Hi, Helen. It's Allison. I — I just wanted to talk to you. I think there's a lot of things I need to say."

The message ended with her phone number and a plea for Helen to call her. As Helen wrote Allison's number on a nearby pad, the machine bleeped again.

"Hi, Helen. It's Frieda. Look, I'm really sorry to bother you. I tried you at home and I didn't know where else to call. It's Jill. She's been arrested."

Chapter Fifteen

The next morning Helen was back at the office trying to gather up newspapers and talk on the phone wedged between ear and shoulder at the same time. On the latest addition to her office — the fashionable futon she'd picked up dirt cheap at a close-out sale — Manny sat, leaning forward, elbows on knees, his attention fixed on the small portable television Helen kept tucked away against the wall.

"I'm glad she's home, Frieda," Helen said as she dropped all the newspapers she'd been stacking together. "No, it's just the newspaper. How is she doing? Well, that's understandable. That was really terrific of Dave to go down there last night. Yes, I think so too. Okay. Okay, I'll call either tonight or tomorrow when — what? Well, Dave said he wants to meet me at his office in Lafayette. I have no idea. All right. Take care, tell Jill I'm thinking of her. 'Bye."

As she hung up Manny turned up the volume with the remote. "Here it is now," he said. Helen took the newspapers with her and sat next to him on the futon.

Another in the endless ranks of perfectly coifed news anchors put on her serious face and started talking about the murder. "Just three days ago — Tuesday, October twenty-seventh — we brought you a story of death and destruction from the suburb of Lafayette. This morning, the drama continues."

"Drama. Jesus," Manny muttered.

"We take you now live to Lafayette, and the Linville clinic."

Helen watched as the reporter, his hair whipping in the wind, stood and spoke from the entrance to the frontage road. A photograph of Cam Logan, probably taken from last year's prom, suddenly filled the screen.

"Yesterday a young life was cut short. The citizens of Lafayette are wondering where it will all end."

A series of questions put to the local residents followed, and then Lieutenant Macabee's freckled face popped into view.

With a snort of disgust, Helen took the remote from Manny's hand and hit the "mute" button. "I've heard all from that man I want to," she said, dropping the remote on the futon and restacking her papers. "It's all the same stuff, anyway — just the teens-in-trouble angle. Not a damned thing."

"Well, remember how it is — it's usually what they don't tell you on TV that's important," Manny offered. He got up and stretched. "Sorry, Sherlock, that's all I have. No one over there is talking much. They want to keep it all to themselves."

"Why? Isn't there enough crime to go around?" Helen snapped.

"It's that Macabee guy. He's got the department so terrified he'll whip major ass that they're almost too scared to fart. I guess he likes being on television, seeing his name in the papers."

"Thanks for trying, anyway." She watched her former partner as he lumbered for the door, noticing again his tired step and red eyes. "Manny, I was going to ask you —"

"Yeah?"

"How's Laurie doing? Is she feeling okay?"

"In answer to your first question, yes. No sickness. In answer to your second question, the one you're not saying out loud, I don't know. Really."

"You haven't decided yet, then?"

He shook his head, looking at the floor, one hand resting on the doorknob. "Not me. Laurie. I told her it was her decision — her body. I told her that I would love to have another child, but that I would support her in her choice. Whatever it is."

Helen bowed her head over the newsprint. Did he mean it? Helen didn't know Laurie well, but she seemed an especially attractive, bright, talented woman who loved her kids and her husband. "Thanks, Manny."

"For what?"

"For telling me about it. For being my gopher. For being my friend."

He smiled and winked at her. "Not bad for a male of the species, huh?"

"As males go." He waved and disappeared through the door. She listened to his footsteps as they faded down the hall and he left the building to start his workday.

Her own workday began shortly after, when she turned off the freeway into Lafayette. Today, however, she wasn't going to the clinic to hold a picket sign and pray. Dave had called her just as she'd gotten home after stopping in the office. "I know it's late, but I'm afraid it can't wait, Helen. We need to talk."

So once again she pulled into the wide circular driveway that graced the Linville home. Built around the turn of the century, when Lafayette was still a one-horse town with barely a general store to its name, the Linville manse had been featured in all sorts of decorator magazines and historical coffee table books. It was only one story high, but that one story was sprawled over an immense space, room after room after room in a Southwestern rustic style that lacked only the theme song from *Bonanza* to make it complete. Helen figured she would have needed a map to live there and navigate her way through the warren of chambers.

Fortunately Dave was there at the door to greet her, posing handsomely in his boots and flannel shirt. An enamel mug steamed in his hand. "Come on in, have some breakfast."

When they were seated at the homey kitchen

table, Helen refused his offer of eggs and toast and waited. She was pretty sure she knew what was coming, but she wanted to hear what he had to say.

"This week's been awful for all of us, Helen," he began, lacing his fingers together on the table. "Both those people — first Melinda, then Reverend Logan's son — I just don't understand it. I guess the poor kid was getting ready to go at it again that night, with his paint and gasoline in that bag." He closed his eyes and sighed. "It just doesn't seem real to me. Then this whole thing with Jill — you've talked to Frieda?"

"Yes, she called me last night. I know she's grateful to you for being there."

"Oh, what else could I do? I just wish this whole mess would get cleared up," he said, as if it were a pile of dirty dishes stacked in a sink. "That's why this is going to be so hard for me to say."

"I'm all ears, Dave."

"Well, the Trustees — they were very interested in what Melinda had to say about the operation of the Linville Clinic. They weren't very pleased."

"And what was that, Dave?"

Shaking his head, he went on, "It's just too much. All the vandalism, those demonstrations, now two deaths — I think they want to shut it down, Helen. After all these years, the Linville will be closing its doors."

"I see." Carmen had warned her last night, although Helen had believed her fears to be exaggerated. "You're trying to tell me my investigation is over, aren't you?"

He smiled ruefully and got up to pour himself

more coffee. With his back to her he said, "Thank you for making it so easy on me, Helen. Jesus, I hate doing this. I think you would have gotten to the bottom of it if you could have had a little more time, but the Trustees — well, they just wouldn't hear of extending your contract any longer."

"It's not a shock, Dave. This is exactly what I expected to hear this morning."

They talked a little longer, ironing out a few details about final payment for services rendered, then Helen got up to go.

Dave shook her hand and looked into her eyes, using his signature "sensitive" expression. "I want to thank you personally, Helen. Jill was absolutely right about you when she suggested you for the job. You've been great, just great."

He ushered her out the door and as she reached her car Helen turned to see him standing on the porch, enamel mug in hand, waving. Helen gazed for a moment, taking in the tableau of the elegant manor, complete with benevolent lord and master fondly seeing her off.

As she pointed the car back toward downtown, Helen told herself that she was only going to call Allison to make sure she was all right. After all, it was the polite thing to do, wasn't it? Allison had called, just as she promised she would. The fact that Helen was in town, close by, able to stop at Allison's house within minutes, had nothing to do with anything. This was strictly on the order of fulfilling an obligation.

At least, that's what Helen told herself as she picked up her cell phone — thank God she'd remembered to put it in the car this morning — and keyed in the number she'd had no trouble memorizing the night before.

"Helen? Is that you?"

"Yeah. How are you? Sorry I didn't call last night, but I got your message so late I didn't want to bother you. So you decided to come home instead of stay at the hotel, after all?"

"That's right." This cheery response was followed by absolute silence.

Helen, paused at a stop light, cast about desperately in her mind for something to say. "So did that potential buyer come through?"

"What?"

"Did that potential buyer come through? The one interested in your house."

"Oh, right. No, it, uh, it didn't work out. Listen, Helen, you don't have to come over. No, really, I insist."

"Huh?" Helen sat frozen at the steering wheel until the car behind her blared its horn and woke her to the fact that the light was green. Mentally cursing the rude driver that peeled around her in a roar of exhaust, Helen drove slowly, finally pulling over next to a gas station. "Allison, what are you talking about?"

"Next week? Yeah, that would be great." She sounded far too chirpy, Helen decided. "It really is all right to pass up on lunch today. You don't have to stop by before you go home."

Jesus. Helen's stomach sank. What she was hearing was a desperate plea for help. Allison needed her there. Now. After the episode in her own kitchen with Bob, Helen knew Allison must be in grave danger.

"Allison, I'm here in Lafayette. I'm calling from my car phone. Just go ahead and talk like we're meeting next week and I'll call the police."

"Thanks, Helen. See you next week. 'Bye." The line went dead. Helen's panic increased when Allison's voice stopped ringing in her ears. She checked for oncoming traffic in her mirror and sped off, breaking all speed limits, while one hand hit numbers on the phone.

By the time she'd rounded the curve in the main road that wound up a hill to Allison's house, she was raging at herself for not calling her last night — not insisting that she stay in the hotel or taking her back to Berkeley, or to a friend's house, or something. Anything but back to Lafayette and Bob. Not far behind she saw flashing lights appear around the bend in the road. No sirens, thank God — they were going to take her seriously this time.

And at least she didn't have to deal with Macabee at the moment. Two black-and-whites pulled up, one swiveling sideways to block the driveway, the other positioned horizontally across the street. At the other end of the circling drive she saw a third police car spanning the street. Two officers with rifles ran up close to the house.

Helen started to get out of her car. "Ma'am, you shouldn't be here!" one of the officers hissed at her. "Get out of the way to safety!"

"I'm the one who called it in. I'm Allison Young's friend —"

"Move, now!" Of course, he was right. Another

man in uniform, his gun drawn, stood behind her, ready to assist her in leaving the vicinity. Helen had done all she could by getting the police here quickly. Now she had to go to the sidelines and wait. She decided to go to the strip mall on the corner, park there and wait as long as Allison might need her. Hopefully it wouldn't be long before —

"Where's the bitch? I want the bitch! Now!"

Helen froze in her tracks for a split second, then dropped down and scrambled around her car until she was hidden from view. Edging her head up slowly, cautiously, she strained to see what was going on.

Bob was forcing Allison's arms behind her back as they stood on the porch. The gun he held to her temple was some kind of automatic — it was hard to tell at this distance what caliber it was. He was dressed in the same clothes he'd worn yesterday. The stubble on his chin was darker, thicker. His eyes blazed out over the lawn to the police cars, searching for something. Or someone.

"Get her out here, now! Or my wife's fucking brains are gonna be all over this fucking yard!"

Very slowly, Helen stood up. Very slowly, Helen walked around her car so Bob could see her. "Here I am, Bob. Why don't you let Allison go and then you and I can talk for a while?" She took a few more steps forward, her legs trembling beneath her and threatening to give way. *Not now,* she ordered herself. No fear. Just concentrate on how to get her away from him. How to get that gun out of his hands.

"You fucking dyke." He started to giggle. "Guess you're not so ready to jump on me now, are you?

What did you do, eat her out the other night and convert her over? Or maybe she was damaged goods all along, huh? I said," he repeated through gritted teeth, "maybe you were damaged goods all along, huh, Al?" The gun's muzzle poked at her temple. Allison blanched white, and her eyes mutely cried out to Helen. She winced as Bob jerked her arms more tightly behind her.

"What is it you want, Bob?" Helen spoke softly, forcing him to pause and listen to her. Behind her she heard the snick of each rifle's safety being released. The police probably had a sharpshooter with his sights trained right at Bob's head, fixing the target in his mind and his vision, waiting for the first opportunity to drill a hole in Bob's brain.

"What do I want?" She was close enough now to smell the stench of his crazed fury. Helen stopped, keeping her arms slightly away from her body so Bob could see her hands, waiting for his response. "I want this bitch —" He jerked her head back, releasing her arms only to grab a fistful of her hair and tug hard — "I want this bitch to die. I want her to suffer like I did when she dumped me."

"Was she the one who dumped you, Bob? Or did you leave her?" Helen asked. "And how have you suffered, Bob?" *Keep saying his name, keep him looking at you, keep him engaged with you.*

"You — you can stand there and look at me and ask that question? You disgusting queer?" The giggling started again. It frightened Helen more than his angry shouts. "My wife — my woman prefers that —" He pointed the gun at Helen — "over the love of a real man."

Everything suddenly sounded very loud in Helen's

ears, although she was sure the cops behind her were frozen still. Each movement of fabric on skin was amplified, each quiet, tense breath, Allison's stifled moans of terror. Helen stared into the steel-gray gun aimed at her head. Odd, how her mind went completely blank. No thoughts, just sensations.

"No." The strangled word came from Allison. Helen looked at the woman on the porch, her head strained backwards, her eyes bright with fear. "No, Bob."

"Look, it talked! The bitch can talk! Now, what did it say? What did Bob's little cunt say?"

"No."

"Is that so?" He grinned, surveyed the scene spread before him. "Well, whatever the little woman wants."

Helen saw it happen as if it took place underwater, distorted and refracted through some strange medium. Bob moved the gun, reversing its position until it was pointed into his mouth. The shot killed him before he fell, sprawled backward against the front door of the house, blood and brains sprayed in a halo behind him. The gun clattered to the porch, accompanied by one piercing scream from Allison, who stood drenched in bright red.

Bob's face was intact. It sagged on the wall, deflated, folded so that he looked as if he were still grinning at Helen.

Chapter Sixteen

Frieda sighed, stepped back from the canvas and studied what she'd just painted. With a grimace she shook her head. "It isn't working. No matter what I do, it isn't working."

Helen, her headache finally fading, wandered around the studio Jill had created out of her attic. The spacious room was lit by a variety of different shades and colors of light, as well as a row of skylights that lined the arched ceiling. Stacked against the walls were a row of canvases in various states of completion. It had always seemed odd to

Helen how Frieda worked on several projects at once and somehow managed to complete all of them. Helen nearly asked what she was working on, then decided against it. She knew that look of utter frustration. When they'd lived together, Helen had joked that seeing that look was like watching a train come down the tracks. Better get the warning signals flashing and jump out of the way.

"Damn." Frieda picked up a large brush from the table next to her, smeared it with thick white paint and slashed a ribbon of white paint across the offending canvas. Helen watched, surprised — Frieda almost never completely destroyed anything she'd worked on. "I can use it later maybe," she used to say.

"Should I get out of here?" Helen asked quietly. "It *is* getting late."

"Is it? I didn't notice the time." Frieda absently wiped her hands with a cloth and looked out of the bank of windows as if for the first time. The sun had gone below the horizon, and the last traces of orange light were fading slowly from the hills separating Berkeley and Contra Costa County. "No light, anyway," Frieda said as she went to the padded bench beneath the windows and plopped down. "Thanks, by the way, for the number of that lawyer."

"No problem. Sherry's great — she'll be good with Jill."

"If she can get Jill to talk," Frieda said with a wry smile.

Helen sat down next to Frieda. They knew each other too well — how could it be otherwise, after sharing their lives for so many years? — for Helen not to know when something serious was wrong. "And thank you for taking Allison in tonight."

Frieda leaned her head against the wall and turned to look at Helen. "Allison is a nice person, Helen. She's lucky to have you."

"Now, hold on! She doesn't 'have' me and I don't 'have' her."

"Right."

"Just so that's understood."

"Right."

"I mean, no confusion about this."

"Not at all." They both started laughing. "Seriously, though, I do like her a lot. I hope she's going to be okay. She can stay here as long as she wants."

"Jill won't mind?"

Frieda got up abruptly from the bench and went back to the canvas. "Right now I haven't the faintest idea what Jill is thinking." She daubed at her palette for a moment, swirling colors around on the stack of paper she kept piled on the table that held paint and brushes. "She won't talk to me."

"What do you mean, she won't talk to you?"

"Just that. She got home from the — the jail, and she just froze me out. She's been in her office at that computer for hours on end, says she's working on a new budget for the Trustees." Frieda dropped the brush and stood staring at the canvas. "I'd understand it if she were trying to find a way to keep her mind off things, but whenever I try to get her to tell me what went on there, what the police did, she won't say a damn thing."

"Sounds like the way I acted, doesn't it?"

Frieda came back to the bench and sat down. "Helen, I'm not pointing fingers and I'm not making comparisons. Really, I'm not."

"I know, honey, I know." Helen leaned back and put her arm around Frieda's shoulders, pulling her close. "It's okay. I guess I was just really seeing how hard I was on you, now that Jill is withdrawing just like I used to."

"Well, one thing is certain. All my talking, all my coaxing, won't do a bit of good. She'll talk when she's ready. I just don't know how much more I can take of this."

Helen got up and stood before the canvas, considering. "You know, Frieda, I think there's some hope for this painting. I wouldn't give up on it yet."

"Think so?" Frieda joined her. "Maybe you're right. I just can't see it, myself."

"That's because you're too close to it. I think you just need some perspective."

"I'll definitely give it some thought." As Helen walked away Frieda picked up a brush, retrieved the palette and stared, rapt, at the ribbon of white paint lacing the canvas.

Helen went down the narrow stairs to the first landing. The house was extremely quiet. It felt empty, although Helen was aware of the people in it — Frieda, busy in her studio, Jill downstairs in the study, Allison asleep at last in the guest bedroom at the end of this corridor. Allison's door was ajar, and Helen headed down the hall. She felt silly, approaching her like a nervous parent checking for the umpteenth time on a sleeping infant. But Helen was unable to wipe the scene of Bob's suicide from her mind. She was worried that Allison would have nightmares, wake up in a strange house and be terrified. It had taken a lot of persuading to get her to take the sedative Jill provided, but the drug was doing its work, Helen decided. She could hear steady breathing coming from the bed. No nightmares yet.

Helen continued walking quietly through the house. The fire had gone out some time ago, and the living room — the same room where she'd seen Melinda Wright for the last time on Monday night — was dark and chill. A few embers still glowed in the fireplace, and Helen thought for a moment about rekindling it, but there was something else she needed to do.

If she remembered correctly, the study was around the corner here, near the side of the house where the garage was. Helen heard Jill clicking away on a keyboard, the letters spilling out furiously. She didn't turn when Helen come in.

One bright lamp burned over Jill's left shoulder, and her silhouette was etched in sharp light and deep shadow. Helen moved closer and peered at the screen.

Jill jumped. "Jesus, I didn't hear you come in."

"Sorry. I just wondered if I could talk to you for a minute."

"Sure." Jill hit a few more keys and turned the chair around to face Helen. "What's up?" Her voice croaked at Helen. She clearly hadn't spoken, to Frieda or anyone else, for hours.

"What are you working on?"

"This? Oh, just some ideas for budgeting for the

clinic. Dave told me the Trustees are just about ready to shut the place down, and I thought maybe I could convince them otherwise."

"Yeah, he said something about it to me when I talked to him today."

Jill nodded. "That's what you wanted to say?"

Helen smiled and shook her head. "I — look, I don't quite know how to do this gracefully."

Jill turned back to the computer. and clicked the mouse several times. "You've been talking to Frieda. Helen, I know you mean well, but this really isn't your business. There's nothing to say. I have to deal with this alone."

"Yep." Helen nodded. "That's what I thought you'd say."

Jill bent her head over the keyboard, fighting to control her irritation. "Helen, if that's all you want, I —

"I knew you'd say it because it's exactly what I would have said." That got Jill to turn around again, and Helen searched that blank, tired face. "I just want you to listen to me. Did Frieda ever talk about why we split up?"

She shook her head. "Helen, I'm not interested in emotional accusations and rehashing the past."

"Neither am I. Do you think this is a lot of fun for me?"

"Then what's the point of —"

"Right now Frieda is up in her studio trying not to fall apart. It's an instant replay of the way I treated her. I kept her cut out of my life. I thought it was the strong thing to do. I thought it made me tough and powerful and capable. Well, bullshit! It didn't make me anything but stupid. You can't keep

170

freezing her out or you'll lose her." Helen stopped herself when she realized how strident she sounded. Jill was right. This was none of her business. "Take it from someone who knows — you'll lose her."

She turned on her heel, not knowing whether to feel angry or embarrassed or relieved that she'd spoken her mind. Jill's soft voice stopped her just as she was closing the door of the study.

"If you understand that feeling, that need to keep things shut down," Jill said, "then you know how difficult it is for me to tell her what happened."

"Then tell me. Give it a shot." Helen sat down on a stool and waited.

Jill sighed, leaned forward on the table and rested her head in her hands. "It was my gun."

Jesus. This was worse than she'd thought. "The gun found with Cam's body?"

"Is that where it was? My God."

Helen stared. Jill looked genuinely shocked. "You're talking about the gun used to kill Melinda Wright?"

"I had no idea — I mean . . ."

"Tell me."

It came spilling out in bits and pieces. Jill knew, from conversations with Frieda about Helen, that violence had been one of several wedges that drove them apart. It was clear from the start that Helen's work, first as a homicide investigator, then as a private detective, had been abhorrent to Frieda.

"I figured if she knew I had a gun, she'd — well, she'd never want to see me again. Not after how much it bothered her when she was with you."

"But why do you have a gun?"

Jill smiled wearily, sitting up to look at Helen. "I

171

guess it was just bulldyke bravado. I got it several years ago, right after I got back from Central America."

"Where you were attacked."

"Right. I think it made me feel stronger, more able to take care of myself."

"I know the feeling," Helen said. "But how the hell did it end up being used on Melinda?"

"If I knew that, I'd be a free woman today, wouldn't I? The really bad part is that I kept it in the clinic." Helen was certain she'd not heard correctly, but Jill nodded and repeated her last statement. "I know, I know, it was a really stupid thing to do, but it seemed like a good idea at the time. I'd been keeping it in the house, but when Frieda moved in I needed to get rid of it, fast. I thought if I put it in the desk, where I could lock it, I'd have it in a safe place until I could get it to a dealer and sell it, or something."

"Did anyone else know about it?"

She shook her head. "No. I didn't want to ruin my politically correct image, you see."

Helen sat upright, thinking hard. Yes, yes, it made sense now — all those bits and pieces that had been circling each other, like the colors on Frieda's palette. But could she prove any of it? Maybe not, since she was dismissed from the investigation and had no real reason to go to the clinic any longer.

"Helen? You're really mad at me, aren't you?"

"What? Oh, Jill, no, I'm not angry. I just have a suggestion."

"I think I can guess what it is, but go ahead."

"Frieda is still in the studio. She's been working

172

all night on a painting. I think she might like some company."

Jill switched off the computer and stood up, twisting her hands together nervously. "Right. You're right, Helen."

"Of course I'm right."

Jill took a deep breath and opened the door, with Helen following close behind. "By the way, Helen, Allison is really a nice person."

"Yeah, so I've been told." Helen watched as Jill went hesitantly up the staircase. Something was missing — violins, perhaps, lilting in the background as the ex-lover bravely sent the wonderful new girlfriend upstairs to the woman they both loved?

Helen stopped for a moment. Did she love Frieda? Still? Yes, she thought, in a way. She always would.

But Allison is such a nice person, Helen grimly reminded herself. With a sigh and a sense of loneliness Helen went to the single guest bed in the spare room behind the study. She knew she wouldn't get much sleep tonight. She prepared herself to be haunted by what she'd just learned from Jill, what she'd just realized about the murders of Melinda and Cam — and haunted by the woman sleeping upstairs.

Chapter Seventeen

The meeting at the church on Saturday morning was a standing-room-only event. Helen squeezed into the back of the building. She was pretty early, so with any luck she'd get to work her way up to the front. No one had thought to turn off the central heating, though, and the place was incredibly stuffy. No one had expected bright warm air to banish the clouds and rain during this final day of October. Predictions were positive for a clear Halloween night.

Thanks to the swift exit of a couple of new mothers carrying wailing infants in their arms through the crowd, Helen found a narrow gap in the aisle halfway toward the front. All around her the congregation was buzzing with tension. Each time a door opened heads turned, necks craning and straining to see who had come in.

Helen wondered if Dave would find out about her presence here. Not that he could order her either to go or stay at the church, but she could already see him looking at her in surprise, one eyebrow raised inquisitively, curious about her motivation for going to this special prayer meeting even though she wasn't officially on the case any longer.

Truth be told, she had had difficulty in rationalizing it herself. Early this morning, before heading back to her own house, she'd sat in Jill and Frieda's kitchen alone with a cup of coffee. No one else was up yet, and Helen wasn't sure what to do about Allison. Should she hang around all day? Did Allison want to go back home for anything? Or to Helen's place?

Irritated at her own indecisiveness, she had gone back to the guest room and started gathering up her things to put them back in the overnight bag she kept packed and ready in the trunk of her car. At least she could be ready to leave at a moment's notice. Then, among the papers stuffed in one of the pockets in the bag, she saw the bright yellow flyer from Dr. Logan's church.

The prayer meeting was held every Saturday morning. So far Helen had managed to avoid them, reasoning to herself that she'd not learn anything useful to her investigation at these gatherings. But now she felt curious. Perhaps because she could simply observe these people, without keeping a critical eye on them and struggling to discern ulterior motives. She sat down on the bed, holding the leaflet and thinking. It was nearly nine o'clock — surely someone would be in the church offices by now?

In answer to her phone call, a young woman with a sweet, high, breathless voice assured her that, yes, the prayer meeting would be held as usual. "It'll be a special service for Cambridge Logan," she breathed.

"Will Dr. Logan be there?"

"Well, I don't know — I mean, it was his son, and all." The voice trailed off in confusion, apparently uncertain of the propriety of Dr. Logan leading a service after suffering such a horrible tragedy. "No," she finally decided, "I doubt very much he'll be there."

What the hell? Helen thought, rummaging through her clothes for something suitable. She couldn't wear jeans, like she got away with for the demonstrations.

Frieda woke up soon after to find Helen fuming over the heap of her clothes in the guest room. "You and Jill are almost the same size, except she's a little taller." Frieda yawned as she led Helen to a long closet off the study. "Look through there."

Helen wasn't surprised at the lack of skirts and dresses. After frantically shoving through rows of hangers and fabric, she found a black suit tucked behind a lab coat. The skirt fit snugly, and it was a bit too long for fashion, but Helen doubted anyone at the church would notice. A pair of stockings, her own plain black loafers and a white Oxford shirt completed the ensemble. Helen pulled up to the drive leading to the church entrance just after nine forty-five.

That had been forty-five minutes ago. The

meeting was to begin, according to the flyer, at ten-thirty, so Helen expectantly watched the doors of the assembly hall, just like everyone else. To her immense relief, no one seemed to find her presence strange. True, the cluster of demonstrators who had come to know her made up only a small portion of the congregation. Most of these faces today were new to Helen.

It was getting hard to breathe. The place was so crowded — no doubt many church members present were making their appearance in Dr. Logan's congregation for the first time in months, succumbing to ghoulish fascination.

Helen was just about to wriggle out of her suit jacket when the vestry door opened and a somber group of men filed out. She stared in surprise at Gary, Donna's fiancé, who led the parade of church elders along the raised platform at the front of the building. Gary wore his suit, so new it shone, with discomfort, unused to the stiff cheap fabric. Donna and a few other women who must have been at the top of the congregation's pecking order demurely followed their men with little, timid steps. Except for Gary, the entire entourage trooped off the platform and took their places in the front pews, which had been roped off pending their arrival.

A ripple of murmurs and whispers wove through the congregation as people made final comments or hissed at their children, or settled more comfortably on the padded pews. Gary strode with purpose to the podium. His hands gripped the sides. He was nervous. Scared shitless, Helen realized.

"Brothers and sisters —" His voice squawked, and the microphone whined. Gary turned his head to the side and coughed, then raised his eyes to some unseen technician who lurked above the congregation in the choir loft. The whining ceased. "Brothers and sisters," he began again, "I talk to you today in sorrow and grief. One of our youngest and most precious brothers, Cambridge Logan, has gone to meet the Lord and is now with the saints in heaven."

Murmured amens followed this. Helen sighed. What on earth ever made her think this would be a good idea? A sort of wrap-up to the investigation? Or maybe she'd fantasized that one final clue, the clue she needed to solve her case, would reveal itself at this meeting.

Gary droned on. Donna's pale, thick blonde hair gleamed as she leaned forward to hear his words. "And I know, brethren, that if Cam were alive today he'd encourage us to go on — to not quit the good fight — to keep on struggling with Satan, like we did this week. He'd tell us to go right ahead, brother, and beat your plowshare into a sword. Go right ahead, sister, and stone those who betray the word of God for the laws of Caesar."

Helen frowned. Obviously, by letting her thoughts wander, she'd missed some crucial turn in Gary's speech. She looked around the room. A variety of reactions could be read on the faces of the church members. Some looked half asleep, in the warmth of the room and under the influence of Gary's monotone. A few were clearly confused, glancing at one another to see if everyone had heard the same words. Still more nodded, faces flushed with righteous indignation, roused at the thought of a crusade.

"I say, we go out and fight for what we know is

right!" Gary was shouting now. The podium rocked beneath his hands clenched on the thin wooden slats. "I say — no, not what I say, but what God says — that we give the devil his due and do away with the sinners who murder the innocent!"

A stunned silence fell over the people listening to Gary. Then, out of the silence, Helen heard it. "Yes," one voice muttered. "Brother Gary is right. Amen, brother."

"Down with Satan and all his followers!"

"The last days are here! The sheep and the goats will be separated, and the chaff blown away from the wheat!"

A few, just a very few, loud voices made themselves heard. For the most part, the crowd watched and listened, as if at a play or in a movie theater. Some looked amazed and sorrowful. The whole object of the meeting — prayer and a memorial to a young boy — had been drowned in rhetoric and invective.

Helen did hear a couple of other voices in the surge of shouting, voices asking for quiet and prayer and pleading for peace. They were too few and too weak, however, to have the slightest effect on the hysteria Helen felt coming to a head in that overcrowded, overheated assembly.

Suddenly Donna sprang to her feet. The crowd hushed as she began the weird chanting Helen had heard before. Arms lifted toward heaven, she turned to face the gathering, and Helen saw tears streaming down her cheeks. Gary watched Donna for a few minutes, then looked back up at the congregation. Helen understood his expression. They were his, and he knew it.

"Who will go with me?" he shouted as soon as Donna had subsided and sank into the welcoming arms of the woman sitting next to her. "Who will follow me to do God's work?"

"What about Dr. Logan?" a man's voice sounded, bellowing through the increasing noise. "What would he have to say about all this?"

"Dr. Logan — Dr. Logan is grieving right now," Gary said, stumbling over the words. "The Lord has sent him a terrible cross to bear. And I know, if he were standing here right now, next to me, he'd say, 'Gary, son, never delay to do the Lord's bidding.'" His eyes blazed and the people stared at him, fascinated. "What about you? And you? And you sitting over there? Are you ready?"

"Yes, Lord, we're ready."

"I said, are you ready?"

The antiphon was repeated back and forth several times. The shouting became frenzied, and people began to stand up.

Gary saw his chance. "Back to the clinic! Back to beat down the devil!"

That was all it took. Helen flattened herself against the wall as people — not all, but many — clambered out of the long pews, kicking and stumbling, rushing out of the church in a mad dash for their cars.

Gary watched with a grin, his features flushed and perspiring, urging them on. "Yes! There's no rest for the saints, for those who love God!"

He walked from the platform, holding a hand out to Donna. She had recovered from her spiritual rigors and once again gazed at Gary with adoring eyes. Sickened by the heat as well as the scene that had just played out before her, Helen slumped into the nearest pew, where a few stragglers who were confused and upset by this militant display sat hunched in misery.

"Helen!"

Great. Donna had spotted her. It was reassuring to know she hadn't blown her cover, Helen thought as Donna rushed over with a beatific smile on her lips, but she didn't think she could stomach a conversation with God's chosen ones at the moment.

"Wasn't he just — just wonderful?" she gushed, glancing back at Gary who waited impatiently in the aisle behind her.

"It was truly amazing," Helen said. "I still can't quite believe it."

"Oh, I know! It's like a miracle — I can still feel the spirit surging in me right now."

"I'm sure you can, Donna. Excuse me, please . . ." Helen got up, fighting down queasiness, and edged out of the pew.

"Aren't you coming, Helen? It will be so wonderful! God will be with us and do great things among us." She reached out for Gary's hand.

Helen saw the flicker of wariness in his eyes. Gary knew exactly what he was doing, playing these people like his own private one-man-band. No doubt he'd play Donna the same way, enjoying himself hugely.

"I have no doubt that amazing things will happen," Helen said as she walked past them. "I won't be there to watch it, though." She strode out of the church, leaving the couple to stare after her. Once outside, Helen gulped down the cold clear air of an October morning.

181

If her own experiences as a child in Mississippi, growing up among people who felt and acted just like this, were valid, then the congregation would soon split up over the issue of peaceful prayer versus militant demonstrations. Dr. Logan might never preach again. Gary would take over the congregation, bulldozing down anyone in his way with sheer brute force.

Helen let her mind play off the various scenarios as she drove back to Jill and Frieda and Allison. To her right, the last traces of dew glittered like jewels on the marble angels in the cemetery.

Chapter Eighteen

Helen marveled at the contrast between the church where she'd spent her morning and the café where she was whiling away the evening. Java Jones had really camped it up for this Halloween. The disappearance of rain, combined with the unusually warm temperatures, had assured Ramona of a good turnout.

"Come on, everyone, grab a mask!" Dressed in black, a fake whip stuck in one back pocket, Ramona was clearly enjoying her role of combination hostess and dominatrix.

Not that everyone who was at Java Jones tonight would get the significance of the whip and the bandanna she sported. Never mind — everyone was going to have a good time tonight, and if they thought the owner and chef of Java Jones was dressed as a rather odd witch, that was just fine.

"I'm already wearing a costume," Helen protested, digging through the box Ramona presented to her as she walked in. "I'm a private eye."

"You know what happens if you don't put on your mask, young lady," Ramona intoned as she flourished her whip.

Helen laughed. Since she'd arrived a bit late — taking too long to decide on an outfit in the hopes that Allison would be there — she didn't have much to choose from. A green grinning skull, a huge beak of a nose on which were propped impossibly large glasses, or the wide green almond eyes of a cat, framed with black fur and whiskers.

"That's the one for me." Helen donned the cat mask and pretended to purr at Ramona.

"Down, kitty! You'll get your Friskies in a minute."

Helen slid the mask off a few minutes later when she spotted Carmen and Gabi, sitting at a table with an elderly couple. Carmen eagerly waved at Helen, then beckoned her over to introduce her to her parents.

They smiled shyly at Helen, then turned to watch events unfold. They spoke in soft Spanish whispers, smiling or chuckling at the variety of costumes that sauntered in.

"You know, I called that lady at El Centro?"

Carmen whispered to Helen. "I think *mi madre y mi padre* will go talk to her soon, too. She's really nice."

"I'm glad I could help, Carmen. Hey, Gabi, how are you?"

Gabi's headdress of bobbing antennae perched on a gold headband waved as she turned to greet Helen. Her smile was hesitant, and Helen decided it was best not to push her into a conversation. With a promise to visit their table later, Helen moved around the room.

As she greeted various guests — it was really interesting to see the number of clinic staff members who'd taken up Ramona's invitation — Helen realized she'd been silly to imagine that Allison would show up. The woman's promises to make it to the party at JJ's had been spoken too soon. Even if she wanted to come, she was probably so traumatized from the events of the past two days that she wouldn't be able to face a noisy crowd. Helen's banter with the guests she knew belied the frustration she felt. She'd have to get over this bullshit. Allison was straight. So what if they'd had a night together? For Allison, it probably meant nothing at all.

"Here, kitty, kitty!" The scent of cigarettes wafted into the room as Dolores came back from taking a smoking break from the party. "How're you doing, Helen?"

"Fine, thanks. Where's your mask?"

"Don't need one. I'm scary enough without it." Dolores gave a gravelly laugh. "Come on, have a seat over here." She led Helen to a tiny table already covered with empty glasses. Dolores had started her party early, Helen realized.

"Hello, Helen." Dave Linville sported a big white Stetson as his costume. He looked a bit relieved to share the burden of entertaining Dolores with Helen, and he pulled a chair up to the tiny table. "Join us."

"For a while. Thanks." Helen sat down. "I take it you heard about what happened at the clinic this morning?" she asked. "Oh — a gin and tonic, please," she said to the waiter hovering nearby.

"They broke a few more windows this time. The police have given up on trying to pretend it's just a bunch of kids, now. Not after — after what's happened." Dave downed his scotch in one gulp, swallowing hard. "Doesn't matter much, anyway," he said in tones too low for Dolores, who was laughing uproariously at the entrance of a particularly strange costume, to hear. "Not if the clinic shuts down."

"So you really think that's what will happen?" Helen watched him signal the waiter.

"Another scotch, please. Yes, I do. Just between you and me, Helen, the Trustees have had it with all this shit at the Linville. I'm not surprised Melinda was going to recommend that it cease operations."

"Say, where are the two lovebirds?" Dolores slurred at Helen. "Your pals, Jill and what's-her-name. The painter, or whatever."

Helen sneaked a wry smile at Dave, then said, "Jill and Frieda wanted to stay home and hand out candy to the kids. I don't think Frieda's had the chance to do that in a long, long time — children just don't go out trick-or-treating in Berkeley anymore."

Dolores nodded sagely. "Not safe, huh?"

Helen let her mind drift again as Dave and Dolores cracked lousy jokes at each other or applauded original costumes when they entered the

186

door. She stared down into her drink, watching the slice of lime floating on the surface. Along with the puzzle pieces that had started falling into place just hours ago, Helen couldn't get Allison out of her thoughts. Where would she go now? Was there some way that Helen could keep in touch with her without crowding her? And what if she was completely off track about the woman, getting her hopes up for nothing? Lord knows, she'd been wrong about straight women before.

"I think it would be good for me to head over to the party. I mean," Allison had said that afternoon, "it's not like sitting around here is keeping me from thinking about Bob and — and what he — I just think it would be nice to be around people."

Helen had studied her thin pale face, the eyes red with tiredness, her voice breaking from exhaustion. It had been hard to fight back the impulse to gather Allison in her arms and comfort her. "Well, if you're sure it's what you want to do. As long as you don't push yourself too hard."

Of course, in spite of her words, Helen had hoped to see her there. She'd dutifully stayed away from Lafayette after getting out of the prayer meeting — going back to her house in Berkeley to take care of an irritated cat, grab a nap and get ready to go to Java Jones. She'd avoided calling Jill or Frieda to check on how Allison was doing. She'd resisted driving by the house to see if Allison had for some reason gone back there. None of it changed her wish to see Allison come through that door, smiling and happy to see her.

The noise didn't bother Helen's thoughts, but silence broke into her brooding. What was going on?

Everyone had stopped talking and laughing, and their eyes were fixed on the entrance to the café. Helen followed their gaze to see who'd just come in.

Dr. Logan had aged overnight. His weak receding chin trembled under a tight drawn mouth. Dark spots breached his face, as if he'd been battered and bruised. Although his eyes were dry right now, they were swollen and red from weeping.

He looked around the room, one hand leaning for support on the doorjamb, the other clutching his Bible to his chest. His eyes rested on Dave and Dolores and Helen at their table in the corner.

In the stillness of the café Dr. Logan walked toward them, his face stony and unreadable, both hands holding the Bible before him like a talisman. "I thought I might find you here tonight," he said, looking at Dave. He barely noticed Helen, who had slipped her mask back on as soon as he walked inside. Dolores looked back and forth between Dave and the minister, her expression one of confusion. Should she laugh or cry at this scene?

"My boy died at your clinic," Dr. Logan said in clear, quiet tones. At this remark Dolores quickly left the table, drink in hand, and headed for the counter where Ramona stood watching everything. To her dismay, Helen was wedged between table and wall, unable to leave without physically moving the table and dislodging the old man, who'd taken the seat vacated by Dolores. "He was killed. The same way those babies are being killed."

Oh, God, he's lost it, Helen thought. Dave saw it, too, and with a glance back at Ramona he hesitantly leaned forward. "Dr. Logan, I know your son died. But it wasn't the Linville that killed him. I know you're in pain, pain beyond anything I could imagine, but —"

The minister's eyes filled with tears. They spilled onto the leather of his Bible with soft plops. "I know God must have a reason for taking him away from us — but I just can't think what it is." He took up his Bible, leafing through the thin pages slowly. "I've looked and looked and looked, and I don't understand. There's no reason for it."

Dave shut his eyes briefly, as if to wipe out the grief released before him. "Dr. Logan, I really think you should go home. Why don't we call you a cab, and —"

"Will you pray with me?" The old man stood up and turned, arms outstretched, to the gaping clientele of the café. "Will you call on the Lord with me, brothers and sisters? Let's get on our knees before God and ask for his mercy. Enlighten us, Lord. So often we do not understand Your ways —"

As if with one voice the costumed patrons looked away, embarrassed at the open display of sorrow. Helen was surprised to find herself near tears. Whatever Dr. Logan believed, he'd been struck by a terrible calamity. Few people would keep from breaking under that strain. She saw Ramona, just inside the kitchen doorway, talking urgently on the phone.

"Hello, Helen."

"Allison?" She couldn't believe it. Allison had gone to some effort for the evening, but no makeup or clothing could hide the strain showing in the lines of her face. Helen squeezed out from behind the table and carefully made a wide berth around the people huddled over the minister, trying to get him to stand

189

up. The buzz of a dozen intense conversations flowed around them as Helen found two seats pushed together at the end of the counter.

"Here I am, ready or not," Allison said. Helen was not deceived. That smile threatened to shatter at any moment.

"I think you should have stayed home. This is too much for you."

"Home? I don't even know where that is anymore." And sure enough the tenuous façade of gaiety cracked open.

"Come on, let's get out of here." Helen spotted the box of masks next to the door. As she tossed the cat's face into the box, she got a glimpse of Dave kneeling next to Dr. Logan, who had finally let himself be persuaded to take a seat. For a moment, the play of light and shadow on Logan's face reminded her strongly of Cam — same sloping chin, beak nose, grayish skin.

Dave must have felt her stare. He looked up and met Helen's eyes as Allison followed her out the door.

"Where to?"

Allison wiped her cheeks and fumbled with her shoulder bag. "Hell if I know. Look, I'm really sorry. This was a mistake. Why don't I just go back to that hotel and —"

"The hell you will. Come on." When Allison hesitated, Helen walked back and stood close to her. "Allison, I have a spare bedroom if you're concerned about my motives. You've been through hell this week, and the last thing I want to do is take advantage of it. Why don't we just go home and see if any kids will come by for candy? I can stand on the porch and do my creepy laugh at them, and you can be the witch who scares their pants off."

Allison considered the proposal. "Do you have any candy at home?" she asked.

"No, but I never get trick-or-treaters, either. Come on. My cat will be ready to kill me for being away so long."

The lighter mood carried them through the streets of Lafayette. Helen drove quickly down Mount Diablo Boulevard, then stopped, confused, at the knot of cars honking and idling several blocks before the freeway entrance.

"What the hell — oh, shit."

"What's wrong?"

"There's a bunch of kids playing around out there." Dressed in vibrant costumes, the revelers — to Helen they looked to be teenagers — had successfully blocked traffic and were dancing to the music blaring from a ghetto blaster someone had placed on a nearby trash container.

"Looks like they're having a good time." Allison smiled at Helen. "I'm sure they'll get out of the way in a minute."

But the minutes crawled by. More boys and girls gathered, costumed and ready to party, ignoring the angry threats of their elders stuck in the middle of the road.

Helen glanced over at Allison. Her face, still and peaceful in the moonlight, gave no indication of her emotions, but Helen didn't want to take chances. "We could try the frontage road," she said carefully. Would the reminder of death be too much for Allison?

"Maybe we should, Helen. It doesn't look like this party is breaking up any time soon."

Helen backed up, steered the car through the closed gas station and headed in the opposite direction. Out of the darkness, beneath the ragged light of street lamps, the Linville Clinic loomed up in white stony splendor. Helen sped past the building and turned right onto the frontage road.

"This shouldn't take long."

"I'm fine, Helen. Really." She smiled and took Helen's hand in a swift, natural gesture of affection that took Helen's breath away.

Hardly daring to move, Helen steered the car carefully through the blackness. The freeway and the BART station stretched out ahead. She wondered again why the city of Lafayette didn't do something about lighting up this damn road. The only thing visible was the BART station, and that stream running to their right could be really dangerous. Normally, the light from the clinic, to their left, wasn't nearly so bright as it was tonight. Then she realized the light pouring in through the back window wasn't coming from the clinic.

"Helen," Allison said nervously.

"I know. We're being followed."

Chapter Nineteen

Helen tugged the steering wheel with all her might and the car swerved to the left, away from the water. A bone-jarring thump heaved her up nearly to the roof of the car.

They must have run over a pile of rocks, Helen decided.

"Stay down," she whispered to Allison. As soon as the headlights had rushed up to them at high speed, she had told Allison to huddle forward. If they were lucky, their pursuer might not have seen her, and

Allison would have a chance to drive away for help if Helen could keep whoever this maniac was occupied.

Helen didn't wait to hear any protests. As soon as she was sure the car wouldn't go anywhere, she climbed out and slammed the door behind her, leaving the headlights on.

"All right," she shouted, "who the fuck is this?"

The other car — she couldn't make out the model behind the glare of those headlights — stopped behind her own vehicle. Helen heard a door slam, heard feet clumping on the road. Silhouetted against the beams, a tall figure with an oddly shaped head stood silent, not moving. Something long dangled from its hand — a pipe?

Helen's stomach sank. Jesus, what had she gotten them into? She stopped herself from glancing back at the car to see if Allison was staying out of sight.

"Why the hell are you hiding from me? Who is that? Too full of shit to show your face?" Even as she shouted the words with a great deal more bravado than she felt, Helen was certain she knew the face behind the mask.

The figure moved closer, weaving in and out of the glaring lights. The thick pipe swung back and forth with each step. Helen could make out the face now — it was the green grinning skull mask from Ramona's grab-bag of costumes, one of the masks Helen had passed over in favor of the cat's eyes.

"Come on, Dave, take that ridiculous thing off. You're not fooling anyone with it."

Dave Linville slowly freed himself of the mask. He dropped it to the ground beside him. "I saw you. Watching me with Logan. I saw the way you stared at me, and I knew then you'd figured it out."

194

"It wasn't that hard, Dave. You told me yourself."

"What the fuck are you talking about?"

Helen instinctively moved back, away from the pipe he was swinging so casually. "Yesterday morning. When I visited you at your house. You talked about Cam and the vandalism."

"So? What does that prove?"

"The police never released any information about the cans of spray paint or the other evidence they found there. I found the body, Dave — that's the only reason I know about it. How did *you* know what they'd found there?"

He stood still. Helen felt his hate in the darkness. "Big fucking deal. It won't matter when I get rid of you."

"You don't think people are going to wonder what's going on when the mall is built where the clinic is now?" Helen, shaking from terror, took a few experimental steps away from the car. If she could just get him away from the car, Allison could get out of there safely.

Dave hadn't moved. He turned, following her, the pipe held tight with both hands now.

"How much money is it, Dave? What are the developers going to give you for this little piece of prime real estate? Isn't the Linville money alone good enough for you?"

"That bitch — I thought Melinda Wright would listen to reason. She stood to make a lot of money, too," he muttered, taking a few steps closer to Helen. "But she wouldn't even hear me out! After the meeting that night, when I followed her back to the clinic, I let her in on the deal. Why should she care about lying to the Trustees? What was it to her?"

"And when she wouldn't go along with your scheme and recommend that the Trustees shut down the Linville, Jill's gun must have come in very handy."

"No, you don't understand." Dave gestured with the pipe, as if explaining something to a small child. Helen heard noises off to the side — maybe Allison was getting ready to get out of there. She took another small step, hoping to distract him from noticing the sound. "I didn't mean to kill her. That part was an accident. I was just going to keep the gun with me after I found it in what was left of Jill's desk. That was actually pretty convenient, you know, those stupid kids throwing that shit in through the window. That gun might have come in handy someday, even just leaving it around. I figured the Trustees would blow up completely if they knew the magnificent Dr. Jill kept a gun in her office."

"So why did you shoot Melinda?"

"She just went on and on — she wouldn't shut up about it. All that bullshit about truth and honesty and her reputation. I guess I took care of her reputation, didn't I?" He laughed. With a cheerful toss he juggled the pipe around in his hands.

Yes, there was definitely something happening in the car. Any minute now Allison could make a run for it.

"It was so fucking easy! I felt like I'd been doing it all my life when she went down in her car. She thought it was just a shortcut, taking this road — a shortcut to hell!"

"I guess it was for Cam too, then."

"Now, that part was bad. I didn't want to do that. But he just wouldn't leave me alone. I had no

196

idea that he'd been out there that night with all his paint and kerosene and shit. The stupid little asshole saw me throw the gun into the creek, and then he gets this bright fucking idea to blackmail me. Me!" Dave laughed and shook his head at the audacity Cam had displayed. "It was so easy, getting him to come out here that night."

"Oh, and you *are* above all that, aren't you, Dave?" Helen felt sick with fear. The car probably wouldn't budge, and Allison would be too afraid to get out. She was going to have to draw Dave farther away.

She started backing up, taunting him as she went. "The mighty Linville, lord of the manor. As long as you get your money, you don't care who dies, do you?"

"That old bag, Ida. My dear old grandmama — she tied it all up so I couldn't get at any of it. Not any real money, just a little here and a little there." Dave was keeping pace with her. Helen kept moving, her car receding into the tight circle of light from Dave's headlights. "What the fuck was I supposed to do, sit around and wait for that fucking check from the Trustees every month? That money is mine. All of it. And you can't stop me from taking it."

Dave raised the pipe over his head with both hands. Helen broke into a run, blindly stumbling over roots and rocks and slipping in mud. She fell forward, stopping just short of landing flat in the creek, both hands squeezing around soft earth still moist from rain. Behind her, Dave panted and cursed as he tangled his way through the weeds. Helen heard him giggle.

"Bye bye, cunt. See you in hell."

The pipe swooshed upward in the air with a humming noise. Helen sprang up, fists full of mud, and lunged at him, smearing the gritty mess into his face. He screamed out, more in surprise than in pain.

Helen was already grubbing on the ground again. By the time Dave regained his balance, she had dug up a sharp-edged rock which she brought swiftly up to his head.

He staggered, moaned, fought to keep his balance while Helen scrambled farther away. If she could get to the BART station — it was a long run, but it was her best hope of getting out of this.

A backward glance told her that her car was still on the rockpile. She couldn't see if Allison had gotten away, but she had other things to worry about.

Dave was moving, circling around Helen. Shit, he was running between her and the BART station. Helen kept going, ignoring the painful stitch in her side, away from the road and the creek. A chain-link fence ahead reflected the dim light from the train pulling into the station. Helen stopped to catch her breath and saw the fence stretching out endlessly over the field. She had no choice but to head for the fence and climb over — Dave would surely smash her head in if she were to try to get to the station.

But he bounded quickly through the field and met her at the fence. She was halfway up before he grabbed her leg. With a scream of anger, she fell back towards him, shoving her foot as hard as she could into what she hoped was his face.

Close enough — it caught him in the throat. He choked and gargled, gasping for air, falling down onto his knees.

"Come on, you bastard!" Helen kicked him,

catching him on the side of the head. She heard the pipe fall down into the grass with a dull thud. "What are you waiting for? Go ahead and beat my fucking brains out!" She kicked again and was rewarded with a whimpering moan.

By then the police cars were screaming along the frontage road, cutting a deep swathe like a row of scythes across the tall grasses by the fence.

Exhausted, Helen fell to her knees next to Dave. He had to be conscious, Helen decided, watching him grope for his pipe.

"There. Go get it, fuckhead." She kicked the pipe over the grass, away from where Dave writhed and moaned.

"Oh my God, Helen, Jesus, did he hurt you?" Allison reached to embrace her, then backed off in fear of hurting something. "Your phone, it was on the floor — I told those damned cops to get their asses over here, he was going to kill you —"

"I'm okay, I'm okay, really." Helen felt all the energy drain from her body, leaving aches and cuts and painful bruises in its wake. "Don't cry, Allison. Please. It's going to be all right."

They waited by the fence, holding each other, for a long time.

Chapter Twenty

It was going to be a dry winter. Helen sat inside the deli and waited for Allison to join her. "What did you get?"

Allison looked at her selection doubtfully. "Eggplant and foccaccia with pesto. Their special today."

Helen laughed. "Wait and see, you'll really like it."

She bit into her own turkey and cheese hungrily. Moving Allison's furniture hadn't taken long, but she was starving after a morning of pulling and pushing and shoving. Most of the heavy stuff was staying with her house in Lafayette, to be used by the new owners.

"Have you got everything you wanted? Any more trips?" she asked.

Allison shook her head, and Helen looked out the window at Piedmont Avenue in Oakland. In spite of the cold weather, the sun had drawn a lot of people out onto the streets. Christmas was only two weeks away, and the shops along the avenue were busy. Allison's apartment building, a quick walk away from the deli where they were eating their lunch, faced south, toward Lake Merritt.

"You should get a lot of light through that front window," Helen said.

"Yeah, I lucked out. In a lot of ways." Allison gave her a big smile.

Helen was right about the sandwich. Allison finished it in record time. "Let's go for a walk," Helen suggested. "Work those kinks out a bit."

They strolled for a while in comfortable silence. To Helen, Allison had gained the best of both worlds by moving into this quiet neighborhood. Like much of Oakland, lower Piedmont maintained the feel of a village even though it was situated only minutes away from downtown Oakland's high-rises and office buildings. Just a bus ride away, in the opposite direction, Berkeley sprawled out in all its garish grungy glory and diversity. Parks and gardens and a lovely man-made lake were all within walking distance.

"It's a great apartment," Helen said. "How did Jill find out about it?"

"I guess it was word of mouth. You know — this

friend told that brother of this co-worker that their fifth cousin twice removed was leaving town."

A shop door opened in front of them. Two women, laughing and holding hands, called a farewell to someone in the store. Christmas carols trilled in the background. "Do you have holiday plans, Allison?"

"No, not really. Jill and Frieda invited me over for dinner. I thought I might take them up on it after I put in a few hours at the clinic."

"So you're back already?"

"Yes, I wanted to be there again. Thank God the Trustees renewed the funding for another five years! That means I'll have a job coordinating volunteer services for at least that long."

Another pair of women stood close together on a street corner. As Allison and Helen passed by, they kissed. Helen watched as Allison stared, then looked away quickly. "They invited me, too."

"I was hoping you'd come."

Helen didn't trust herself to say more at this point. In the past two months, as she and Allison slowly got to know each other, Helen saw with increasing clarity just how important Allison was to her. Whether she liked it or not, she knew it was love, rearing its ugly head again. So far, she'd been very cautious to conceal her feelings. Every time Helen felt encouraged to reveal those emotions, she remembered all that Allison had been through and shrank from putting any pressure on her fragile composure.

"Hey, where'd you go, Helen?"

"What? Oh, I'm sorry." They were already standing in front of Allison's apartment building.

"I was asking if you'd like to come upstairs again. Just for a minute."

"Sure." Maybe there was something else that needed unpacking. Helen didn't want to overstay her welcome — she'd make an exit pretty soon.

Allison threw open the windows, letting cool air rush in. Helen stood awkwardly in the middle of the empty living room and watched Allison moving around her new home.

"Do you think you'll miss the house? Or Lafayette? I mean, this is such a huge change for you, being here."

"Miss it? Hell, no!" She shuddered, standing by the window and looking out over the street where they'd just walked. "I feel so different here. So —"

"What?" Helen walked closer. The afternoon sun slanted into Allison's eyes, lighting the dark green into soft gold.

"So free. Completely free. Like anything is possible." She smiled down at the street.

"Anything *is* possible, Allison. Including your happiness." *Which I want more than anything in the world.*

"Does that include you, Helen? Are you — are we — a possibility?"

Helen froze. She watched Allison's profile, which carved out a delicate shadow on the curtains. "Possibly."

Allison reached a hand to Helen without looking at her. Helen took it, held it lightly in both her own, then pulled Allison close. They leaned together, enjoying the warmth, the intimacy they'd both missed for so long.

"I've started therapy again. You know, I've been wanting to ask Dr. Whitt — that's her name, Grace Whitt — if she's a lesbian."

"Why don't you?"

"Are you kidding? We'd have to process that!"

"Right, how silly of me." They laughed at their own silliness, then Helen said, "I just haven't wanted to crowd you. I mean, you've had so much to deal with. Bob, the move, the whole awful mess at the clinic — the last thing you needed was some insensitive dyke mooning after you."

"Hm. That doesn't sound so bad."

Helen's lips brushed Allison's hair and she tightened her embrace. "Like I said, sweetheart, anything is possible."

"Good enough for now."

Maybe it was her imagination, but Helen could have sworn she could see all the way out to San Francisco Bay that night as she drove, several hours later, back to her home in Berkeley. Allison's touch, her voice, lingered in Helen's thoughts like the lights strung on the Bay Bridge, bright points of longing and hope.

Anything was possible — even love.

A few of the publications of
THE NAIAD PRESS, INC.
P.O. Box 10543 • Tallahassee, Florida 32302
Phone (904) 539-5965
Toll-Free Order Number: 1-800-533-1973
Mail orders welcome. Please include 15% postage.
Write or call for our free catalog which also features an
incredible selection of lesbian videos.

SMOKE AND MIRRORS by Pat Welch. 224 pp. 5th Helen Black
Mystery. ISBN 1-56280-143-0 $10.95

DANCING IN THE DARK edited by Barbara Grier & Christine
Cassidy. 272 pp. Erotic love stories by Naiad Press authors.
ISBN 1-56280-144-9 14.95

TIME AND TIME AGAIN by Catherine Ennis. 176 pp. Passionate
love affair. ISBN 1-56280-145-7 10.95

INNER CIRCLE by Claire McNab. 208 pp. 8th Carol Ashton
Mystery. ISBN 1-56280-135-X 10.95

LESBIAN SEX: AN ORAL HISTORY by Susan Johnson.
240 pp. Need we say more? ISBN 1-56280-142-2 14.95

BABY, IT'S COLD by Jaye Maiman. 256 pp. 5th Robin Miller
Mystery. ISBN 1-56280-141-4 19.95

WILD THINGS by Karin Kallmaker. 240 pp. By the undisputed
mistress of lesbian romance. ISBN 1-56280-139-2 10.95

THE GIRL NEXT DOOR by Mindy Kaplan. 208 pp. Just what
you'd expect. ISBN 1-56280-140-6 10.95

NOW AND THEN by Penny Hayes. 240 pp. Romance on the
westward journey. ISBN 1-56280-121-X 10.95

HEART ON FIRE by Diana Simmonds. 176 pp. The romantic and
erotic rival of *Curious Wine*. ISBN 1-56280-152-X 10.95

DEATH AT LAVENDER BAY by Lauren Wright Douglas. 208 pp.
1st Allison O'Neil Mystery. ISBN 1-56280-085-X 10.95

YES I SAID YES I WILL by Judith McDaniel. 272 pp. Hot
romance by famous author. ISBN 1-56280-138-4 10.95

FORBIDDEN FIRES by Margaret C. Anderson. Edited by Mathilda
Hills. 176 pp. Famous author's "unpublished" Lesbian romance.
ISBN 1-56280-123-6 21.95

SIDE TRACKS by Teresa Stores. 160 pp. Gender-bending
Lesbians on the road. ISBN 1-56280-122-8 10.95

HOODED MURDER by Annette Van Dyke. 176 pp. 1st Jessie
Batelle Mystery. ISBN 1-56280-134-1   10.95

WILDWOOD FLOWERS by Julia Watts. 208 pp. Hilarious and
heart-warming tale of true love. ISBN 1-56280-127-9   10.95

NEVER SAY NEVER by Linda Hill. 224 pp. Rule #1: Never get involved
with . . . ISBN 1-56280-126-0   10.95

THE SEARCH by Melanie McAllester. 240 pp. Exciting top cop
Tenny Mendoza case. ISBN 1-56280-150-3   10.95

THE WISH LIST by Saxon Bennett. 192 pp. Romance through
the years. ISBN 1-56280-125-2   10.95

FIRST IMPRESSIONS by Kate Calloway. 208 pp. P.I. Cassidy
James' first case. ISBN 1-56280-133-3   10.95

OUT OF THE NIGHT by Kris Bruyer. 192 pp. Spine-tingling
thriller. ISBN 1-56280-120-1   10.95

NORTHERN BLUE by Tracey Richardson. 224 pp. Police recruits
Miki & Miranda — passion in the line of fire. ISBN 1-56280-118-X   10.95

LOVE'S HARVEST by Peggy J. Herring. 176 pp. by the author of
Once More With Feeling. ISBN 1-56280-117-1   10.95

THE COLOR OF WINTER by Lisa Shapiro. 208 pp. Romantic
love beyond your wildest dreams. ISBN 1-56280-116-3   10.95

FAMILY SECRETS by Laura DeHart Young. 208 pp. Enthralling
romance and suspense. ISBN 1-56280-119-8   10.95

INLAND PASSAGE by Jane Rule. 288 pp. Tales exploring conven-
tional & unconventional relationships. ISBN 0-930044-56-8   10.95

DOUBLE BLUFF by Claire McNab. 208 pp. 7th Carol Ashton
Mystery. ISBN 1-56280-096-5   10.95

BAR GIRLS by Lauran Hoffman. 176 pp. See the movie, read
the book! ISBN 1-56280-115-5   10.95

THE FIRST TIME EVER edited by Barbara Grier & Christine
Cassidy. 272 pp. Love stories by Naiad Press authors.
ISBN 1-56280-086-8   14.95

MISS PETTIBONE AND MISS McGRAW by Brenda Weathers.
208 pp. A charming ghostly love story. ISBN 1-56280-151-1   10.95

CHANGES by Jackie Calhoun. 208 pp. Involved romance and
relationships. ISBN 1-56280-083-3   10.95

FAIR PLAY by Rose Beecham. 256 pp. 3rd Amanda Valentine
Mystery. ISBN 1-56280-081-7   10.95

PAXTON COURT by Diane Salvatore. 256 pp. Erotic and wickedly
funny contemporary tale about the business of learning to live
together. ISBN 1-56280-109-0   21.95

PAYBACK by Celia Cohen. 176 pp. A gripping thriller of romance,
revenge and betrayal. ISBN 1-56280-084-1   10.95

THE BEACH AFFAIR by Barbara Johnson. 224 pp. Sizzling
summer romance/mystery/intrigue.   ISBN 1-56280-090-6   10.95

GETTING THERE by Robbi Sommers. 192 pp. Nobody does it
like Robbi!   ISBN 1-56280-099-X   10.95

FINAL CUT by Lisa Haddock. 208 pp. 2nd Carmen Ramirez
Mystery.   ISBN 1-56280-088-4   10.95

FLASHPOINT by Katherine V. Forrest. 256 pp. A Lesbian
blockbuster!   ISBN 1-56280-079-5   10.95

CLAIRE OF THE MOON by Nicole Conn. Audio Book —Read
by Marianne Hyatt.   ISBN 1-56280-113-9   16.95

FOR LOVE AND FOR LIFE: INTIMATE PORTRAITS OF
LESBIAN COUPLES by Susan Johnson. 224 pp.
                                          ISBN 1-56280-091-4   14.95

DEVOTION by Mindy Kaplan. 192 pp. See the movie — read
the book!   ISBN 1-56280-093-0   10.95

SOMEONE TO WATCH by Jaye Maiman. 272 pp. 4th Robin
Miller Mystery.   ISBN 1-56280-095-7   10.95

GREENER THAN GRASS by Jennifer Fulton. 208 pp. A young
woman — a stranger in her bed.   ISBN 1-56280-092-2   10.95

TRAVELS WITH DIANA HUNTER by Regine Sands. Erotic
lesbian romp. Audio Book (2 cassettes)   ISBN 1-56280-107-4   16.95

CABIN FEVER by Carol Schmidt. 256 pp. Sizzling suspense
and passion.   ISBN 1-56280-089-1   10.95

THERE WILL BE NO GOODBYES by Laura DeHart Young. 192
pp. Romantic love, strength, and friendship.   ISBN 1-56280-103-1   10.95

FAULTLINE by Sheila Ortiz Taylor. 144 pp. Joyous comic
lesbian novel.   ISBN 1-56280-108-2   9.95

OPEN HOUSE by Pat Welch. 176 pp. 4th Helen Black Mystery.
                                          ISBN 1-56280-102-3   10.95

ONCE MORE WITH FEELING by Peggy J. Herring. 240 pp.
Lighthearted, loving romantic adventure. ISBN 1-56280-089-2   10.95

FOREVER by Evelyn Kennedy. 224 pp. Passionate romance — love
overcoming all obstacles.   ISBN 1-56280-094-9   10.95

WHISPERS by Kris Bruyer. 176 pp. Romantic ghost story
                                          ISBN 1-56280-082-5   10.95

NIGHT SONGS by Penny Mickelbury. 224 pp. 2nd Gianna Maglione
Mystery.   ISBN 1-56280-097-3   10.95

GETTING TO THE POINT by Teresa Stores. 256 pp. Classic
southern Lesbian novel.   ISBN 1-56280-100-7   10.95

PAINTED MOON by Karin Kallmaker. 224 pp. Delicious
Kallmaker romance.   ISBN 1-56280-075-2   10.95

THE MYSTERIOUS NAIAD edited by Katherine V. Forrest & Barbara Grier. 320 pp. Love stories by Naiad Press authors.
ISBN 1-56280-074-4   14.95

DAUGHTERS OF A CORAL DAWN by Katherine V. Forrest. 240 pp. Tenth Anniversay Edition.   ISBN 1-56280-104-X   10.95

BODY GUARD by Claire McNab. 208 pp. 6th Carol Ashton Mystery.   ISBN 1-56280-073-6   10.95

CACTUS LOVE by Lee Lynch. 192 pp. Stories by the beloved storyteller.   ISBN 1-56280-071-X   9.95

SECOND GUESS by Rose Beecham. 216 pp. 2nd Amanda Valentine Mystery.   ISBN 1-56280-069-8   9.95

THE SURE THING by Melissa Hartman. 208 pp. L.A. earthquake romance.   ISBN 1-56280-078-7   9.95

A RAGE OF MAIDENS by Lauren Wright Douglas. 240 pp. 6th Caitlin Reece Mystery.   ISBN 1-56280-068-X   10.95

TRIPLE EXPOSURE by Jackie Calhoun. 224 pp. Romantic drama involving many characters.   ISBN 1-56280-067-1   10.95

UP, UP AND AWAY by Catherine Ennis. 192 pp. Delightful romance.   ISBN 1-56280-065-5   9.95

PERSONAL ADS by Robbi Sommers. 176 pp. Sizzling short stories.   ISBN 1-56280-059-0   10.95

FLASHPOINT by Katherine V. Forrest. 256 pp. Lesbian blockbuster!   ISBN 1-56280-043-4   22.95

CROSSWORDS by Penny Sumner. 256 pp. 2nd Victoria Cross Mystery.   ISBN 1-56280-064-7   9.95

SWEET CHERRY WINE by Carol Schmidt. 224 pp. A novel of suspense.   ISBN 1-56280-063-9   9.95

CERTAIN SMILES by Dorothy Tell. 160 pp. Erotic short stories.
ISBN 1-56280-066-3   9.95

EDITED OUT by Lisa Haddock. 224 pp. 1st Carmen Ramirez Mystery.   ISBN 1-56280-077-9   9.95

WEDNESDAY NIGHTS by Camarin Grae. 288 pp. Sexy adventure.   ISBN 1-56280-060-4   10.95

SMOKEY O by Celia Cohen. 176 pp. Relationships on the playing field.   ISBN 1-56280-057-4   9.95

KATHLEEN O'DONALD by Penny Hayes. 256 pp. Rose and Kathleen find each other and employment in 1909 NYC.
ISBN 1-56280-070-1   9.95

STAYING HOME by Elisabeth Nonas. 256 pp. Molly and Alix want a baby . . . or do they?   ISBN 1-56280-076-0   10.95

TRUE LOVE by Jennifer Fulton. 240 pp. Six lesbians searching for love in all the "right" places.   ISBN 1-56280-035-3   10.95

GARDENIAS WHERE THERE ARE NONE by Molleen Zanger. 176 pp. Why is Melanie inextricably drawn to the old house?
ISBN 1-56280-056-6   9.95

KEEPING SECRETS by Penny Mickelbury. 208 pp. 1st Gianna Maglione Mystery.   ISBN 1-56280-052-3   9.95

THE ROMANTIC NAIAD edited by Katherine V. Forrest & Barbara Grier. 336 pp. Love stories by Naiad Press authors.
ISBN 1-56280-054-X   14.95

UNDER MY SKIN by Jaye Maiman. 336 pp. 3rd Robin Miller Mystery.   ISBN 1-56280-049-3.   10.95

CAR POOL by Karin Kallmaker. 272pp. Lesbians on wheels and then some!   ISBN 1-56280-048-5   10.95

NOT TELLING MOTHER: STORIES FROM A LIFE by Diane Salvatore. 176 pp. Her 3rd novel.   ISBN 1-56280-044-2   9.95

GOBLIN MARKET by Lauren Wright Douglas. 240pp. 5th Caitlin Reece Mystery.   ISBN 1-56280-047-7   10.95

LONG GOODBYES by Nikki Baker. 256 pp. 3rd Virginia Kelly Mystery.   ISBN 1-56280-042-6   9.95

FRIENDS AND LOVERS by Jackie Calhoun. 224 pp. Midwestern Lesbian lives and loves.   ISBN 1-56280-041-8   10.95

THE CAT CAME BACK by Hilary Mullins. 208 pp. Highly praised Lesbian novel.   ISBN 1-56280-040-X   9.95

BEHIND CLOSED DOORS by Robbi Sommers. 192 pp. Hot, erotic short stories.   ISBN 1-56280-039-6   9.95

CLAIRE OF THE MOON by Nicole Conn. 192 pp. See the movie — read the book!   ISBN 1-56280-038-8   10.95

SILENT HEART by Claire McNab. 192 pp. Exotic Lesbian romance.   ISBN 1-56280-036-1   10.95

HAPPY ENDINGS by Kate Brandt. 272 pp. Intimate conversations with Lesbian authors.   ISBN 1-56280-050-7   10.95

THE SPY IN QUESTION by Amanda Kyle Williams. 256 pp. 4th Madison McGuire Mystery.   ISBN 1-56280-037-X   9.95

SAVING GRACE by Jennifer Fulton. 240 pp. Adventure and romantic entanglement.   ISBN 1-56280-051-5   10.95

THE YEAR SEVEN by Molleen Zanger. 208 pp. Women surviving in a new world.   ISBN 1-56280-034-5   9.95

CURIOUS WINE by Katherine V. Forrest. 176 pp. Tenth Anniversary Edition. The most popular contemporary Lesbian love story.
ISBN 1-56280-053-1   10.95
     Audio Book (2 cassettes)   ISBN 1-56280-105-8   16.95

CHAUTAUQUA by Catherine Ennis. 192 pp. Exciting, romantic adventure.   ISBN 1-56280-032-9   9.95

A SINGULAR SPY by Amanda K. Williams. 192 pp. 3rd
Madison McGuire Mystery.   ISBN 1-56280-008-6   8.95

THE END OF APRIL by Penny Sumner. 240 pp. 1st Victoria
Cross Mystery.   ISBN 1-56280-007-8   8.95

HOUSTON TOWN by Deborah Powell. 208 pp. A Hollis
Carpenter Mystery.   ISBN 1-56280-006-X   8.95

KISS AND TELL by Robbi Sommers. 192 pp. Scorching stories
by the author of *Pleasures*.   ISBN 1-56280-005-1   10.95

STILL WATERS by Pat Welch. 208 pp. 2nd Helen Black Mystery.
          ISBN 0-941483-97-5   9.95

TO LOVE AGAIN by Evelyn Kennedy. 208 pp. Wildly romantic
love story.   ISBN 0-941483-85-1   9.95

IN THE GAME by Nikki Baker. 192 pp. 1st Virginia Kelly
Mystery.   ISBN 1-56280-004-3   9.95

AVALON by Mary Jane Jones. 256 pp. A Lesbian Arthurian
romance.   ISBN 0-941483-96-7   9.95

STRANDED by Camarin Grae. 320 pp. Entertaining, riveting
adventure.   ISBN 0-941483-99-1   9.95

THE DAUGHTERS OF ARTEMIS by Lauren Wright Douglas.
240 pp. 3rd Caitlin Reece Mystery.   ISBN 0-941483-95-9   9.95

CLEARWATER by Catherine Ennis. 176 pp. Romantic secrets
of a small Louisiana town.   ISBN 0-941483-65-7   8.95

THE HALLELUJAH MURDERS by Dorothy Tell. 176 pp. 2nd
Poppy Dillworth Mystery.   ISBN 0-941483-88-6   8.95

SECOND CHANCE by Jackie Calhoun. 256 pp. Contemporary
Lesbian lives and loves.   ISBN 0-941483-93-2   9.95

BENEDICTION by Diane Salvatore. 272 pp. Striking, contemporary romantic novel.   ISBN 0-941483-90-8   9.95

BLACK IRIS by Jeane Harris. 192 pp. Caroline's hidden past . . .
          ISBN 0-941483-68-1   8.95

TOUCHWOOD by Karin Kallmaker. 240 pp. Loving, May/
December romance.   ISBN 0-941483-76-2   9.95

COP OUT by Claire McNab. 208 pp. 4th Carol Ashton Mystery.
          ISBN 0-941483-84-3   10.95

THE BEVERLY MALIBU by Katherine V. Forrest. 288 pp. 3rd
Kate Delafield Mystery.   ISBN 0-941483-48-7   11.95

THAT OLD STUDEBAKER by Lee Lynch. 272 pp. Andy's affair
with Regina and her attachment to her beloved car.
          ISBN 0-941483-82-7   9.95

PASSION'S LEGACY by Lori Paige. 224 pp. Sarah is swept into
the arms of Augusta Pym in this delightful historical romance.
          ISBN 0-941483-81-9   8.95

THE PROVIDENCE FILE by Amanda Kyle Williams. 256 pp.
2nd Madison McGuire Mystery.   ISBN 0-941483-92-4   8.95

I LEFT MY HEART by Jaye Maiman. 320 pp. 1st Robin Miller
Mystery.   ISBN 0-941483-72-X   10.95

THE PRICE OF SALT by Patricia Highsmith (writing as Claire
Morgan). 288 pp. Classic lesbian novel, first issued in 1952 . . .
acknowledged by its author under her own, very famous, name.
                                      ISBN 1-56280-003-5   9.95

SIDE BY SIDE by Isabel Miller. 256 pp. From beloved author of
Patience and Sarah.   ISBN 0-941483-77-0   10.95

STAYING POWER: LONG TERM LESBIAN COUPLES by
Susan E. Johnson. 352 pp. Joys of coupledom. ISBN 0-941-483-75-4   14.95

SLICK by Camarin Grae. 304 pp. Exotic, erotic adventure.
                                      ISBN 0-941483-74-6   9.95

NINTH LIFE by Lauren Wright Douglas. 256 pp. 2nd Caitlin
Reece Mystery.   ISBN 0-941483-50-9   8.95

PLAYERS by Robbi Sommers. 192 pp. Sizzling, erotic novel.
                                      ISBN 0-941483-73-8   9.95

MURDER AT RED ROOK RANCH by Dorothy Tell. 224 pp.
1st Poppy Dillworth Mystery.   ISBN 0-941483-80-0   8.95

A ROOM FULL OF WOMEN by Elisabeth Nonas. 256 pp.
Contemporary Lesbian lives.   ISBN 0-941483-69-X   9.95

THEME FOR DIVERSE INSTRUMENTS by Jane Rule. 208 pp.
Powerful romantic lesbian stories.   ISBN 0-941483-63-0   8.95

CLUB 12 by Amanda Kyle Williams. 288 pp. Espionage thriller
featuring a lesbian agent!   ISBN 0-941483-64-9   8.95

DEATH DOWN UNDER by Claire McNab. 240 pp. 3rd Carol
Ashton Mystery.   ISBN 0-941483-39-8   9.95

MONTANA FEATHERS by Penny Hayes. 256 pp. Vivian and
Elizabeth find love in frontier Montana. ISBN 0-941483-61-4   8.95

LIFESTYLES by Jackie Calhoun. 224 pp. Contemporary Lesbian
lives and loves.   ISBN 0-941483-57-6   10.95

WILDERNESS TREK by Dorothy Tell. 192 pp. Six women on
vacation learning "new" skills.   ISBN 0-941483-60-6   8.95

MURDER BY THE BOOK by Pat Welch. 256 pp. 1st Helen
Black Mystery.   ISBN 0-941483-59-2   9.95

THERE'S SOMETHING I'VE BEEN MEANING TO TELL YOU
Ed. by Loralee MacPike. 288 pp. Gay men and lesbians coming out
to their children.   ISBN 0-941483-44-4   9.95

LIFTING BELLY by Gertrude Stein. Ed. by Rebecca Mark. 104 pp.
Erotic poetry.   ISBN 0-941483-51-7   10.95

AFTER THE FIRE by Jane Rule. 256 pp. Warm, human novel by
this incomparable author. ISBN 0-941483-45-2   8.95

PLEASURES by Robbi Sommers. 204 pp. Unprecedented
eroticism. ISBN 0-941483-49-5   8.95

EDGEWISE by Camarin Grae. 372 pp. Spellbinding
adventure. ISBN 0-941483-19-3   9.95

FATAL REUNION by Claire McNab. 224 pp. 2nd Carol Ashton
Mystery. ISBN 0-941483-40-1   10.95

IN EVERY PORT by Karin Kallmaker. 228 pp. Jessica's sexy,
adventuresome travels. ISBN 0-941483-37-7   10.95

OF LOVE AND GLORY by Evelyn Kennedy. 192 pp. Exciting
WWII romance. ISBN 0-941483-32-0   10.95

CLICKING STONES by Nancy Tyler Glenn. 288 pp. Love
transcending time. ISBN 0-941483-31-2   9.95

SOUTH OF THE LINE by Catherine Ennis. 216 pp. Civil War
adventure. ISBN 0-941483-29-0   8.95

WOMAN PLUS WOMAN by Dolores Klaich. 300 pp. Supurb
Lesbian overview. ISBN 0-941483-28-2   9.95

THE FINER GRAIN by Denise Ohio. 216 pp. Brilliant young
college lesbian novel. ISBN 0-941483-11-8   8.95

OCTOBER OBSESSION by Meredith More. Josie's rich, secret
Lesbian life. ISBN 0-941483-18-5   8.95

BEFORE STONEWALL: THE MAKING OF A GAY AND
LESBIAN COMMUNITY by Andrea Weiss & Greta Schiller.
96 pp., 25 illus. ISBN 0-941483-20-7   7.95

OSTEN'S BAY by Zenobia N. Vole. 204 pp. Sizzling adventure
romance set on Bonaire. ISBN 0-941483-15-0   8.95

LESSONS IN MURDER by Claire McNab. 216 pp. 1st Carol Ashton
Mystery. ISBN 0-941483-14-2   10.95

YELLOWTHROAT by Penny Hayes. 240 pp. Margarita, bandit,
kidnaps Julia. ISBN 0-941483-10-X   8.95

SAPPHISTRY: THE BOOK OF LESBIAN SEXUALITY by
Pat Califia. 3d edition, revised. 208 pp. ISBN 0-941483-24-X   10.95

CHERISHED LOVE by Evelyn Kennedy. 192 pp. Erotic Lesbian
love story. ISBN 0-941483-08-8   10.95

THE SECRET IN THE BIRD by Camarin Grae. 312 pp. Striking,
psychological suspense novel. ISBN 0-941483-05-3   8.95

TO THE LIGHTNING by Catherine Ennis. 208 pp. Romantic
Lesbian 'Robinson Crusoe' adventure. ISBN 0-941483-06-1   8.95

DREAMS AND SWORDS by Katherine V. Forrest. 192 pp.
Romantic, erotic, imaginative stories. ISBN 0-941483-03-7   10.95

MEMORY BOARD by Jane Rule. 336 pp. Memorable novel
about an aging Lesbian couple.   ISBN 0-941483-02-9   12.95

THE ALWAYS ANONYMOUS BEAST by Lauren Wright Douglas.
224 pp. 1st Caitlin Reece Mystery.
                  ISBN 0-941483-04-5   8.95

THE BLACK AND WHITE OF IT by Ann Allen Shockley.
144 pp. Short stories.   ISBN 0-930044-96-7   7.95

SAY JESUS AND COME TO ME by Ann Allen Shockley. 288
pp. Contemporary romance.   ISBN 0-930044-98-3   8.95

MURDER AT THE NIGHTWOOD BAR by Katherine V. Forrest.
240 pp. 2nd Kate Delafield Mystery.   ISBN 0-930044-92-4   11.95

WINGED DANCER by Camarin Grae. 228 pp. Erotic Lesbian
adventure story.   ISBN 0-930044-88-6   8.95

PAZ by Camarin Grae. 336 pp. Romantic Lesbian adventurer
with the power to change the world.   ISBN 0-930044-89-4   8.95

SOUL SNATCHER by Camarin Grae. 224 pp. A puzzle, an
adventure, a mystery — Lesbian romance.   ISBN 0-930044-90-8   8.95

THE LOVE OF GOOD WOMEN by Isabel Miller. 224 pp.
Long-awaited new novel by the author of the beloved *Patience
and Sarah.*   ISBN 0-930044-81-9   8.95

THE HOUSE AT PELHAM FALLS by Brenda Weathers. 240
pp. Suspenseful Lesbian ghost story.   ISBN 0-930044-79-7   7.95

PEMBROKE PARK by Michelle Martin. 256 pp. Derring-do
and daring romance in Regency England.   ISBN 0-930044-77-0   7.95

THE LONG TRAIL by Penny Hayes. 248 pp. Vivid adventures
of two women in love in the old west.   ISBN 0-930044-76-2   8.95

AN EMERGENCE OF GREEN by Katherine V. Forrest. 288
pp. Powerful novel of sexual discovery.   ISBN 0-930044-69-X   11.95

THE LESBIAN PERIODICALS INDEX edited by Claire Potter.
432 pp. Author & subject index.   ISBN 0-930044-74-6   12.95

DESERT OF THE HEART by Jane Rule. 224 pp. A classic;
basis for the movie *Desert Hearts.*   ISBN 0-930044-73-8   10.95

TORCHLIGHT TO VALHALLA by Gale Wilhelm. 128 pp.
Classic novel by a great Lesbian writer.   ISBN 0-930044-68-1   7.95

LESBIAN NUNS: BREAKING SILENCE edited by Rosemary
Curb and Nancy Manahan. 432 pp. Unprecedented autobiographies
of religious life.   ISBN 0-930044-62-2   9.95

SEX VARIANT WOMEN IN LITERATURE by Jeannette
Howard Foster. 448 pp. Literary history.   ISBN 0-930044-65-7   8.95

A HOT-EYED MODERATE by Jane Rule. 252 pp. Hard-hitting
essays on gay life; writing; art.   ISBN 0-930044-57-6   7.95

AMATEUR CITY by Katherine V. Forrest. 224 pp. 1st Kate
Delafield Mystery.   ISBN 0-930044-55-X   10.95

THE SOPHIE HOROWITZ STORY by Sarah Schulman. 176 pp.
Engaging novel of madcap intrigue.   ISBN 0-930044-54-1   7.95

THE YOUNG IN ONE ANOTHER'S ARMS by Jane Rule.
224 pp. Classic Jane Rule.   ISBN 0-930044-53-3   9.95

AGAINST THE SEASON by Jane Rule. 224 pp. Luminous,
complex novel of interrelationships.   ISBN 0-930044-48-7   8.95

LOVERS IN THE PRESENT AFTERNOON by Kathleen Fleming.
288 pp. A novel about recovery and growth. ISBN 0-930044-46-0   8.95

CONTRACT WITH THE WORLD by Jane Rule. 340 pp. Powerful, panoramic novel of gay life.   ISBN 0-930044-28-2   9.95

THIS IS NOT FOR YOU by Jane Rule. 284 pp. A letter to a
beloved is also an intricate novel.   ISBN 0-930044-25-8   8.95

OUTLANDER by Jane Rule. 207 pp. Short stories and essays by
one of our finest writers.   ISBN 0-930044-17-7   8.95

ODD GIRL OUT by Ann Bannon.   ISBN 0-930044-83-5   5.95
I AM A WOMAN 84-3; WOMEN IN THE SHADOWS 85-1;   each
JOURNEY TO A WOMAN 86-X; BEEBO BRINKER 87-8. Golden
oldies about life in Greenwich Village.

JOURNEY TO FULFILLMENT, A WORLD WITHOUT MEN, and   3.95
RETURN TO LESBOS. All by Valerie Taylor   each

These are just a few of the many Naiad Press titles — we are the oldest and largest lesbian/feminist publishing company in the world. We also offer an enormous selection of lesbian video products. Please request a complete catalog. We offer personal service; we encourage and welcome direct mail orders from individuals who have limited access to bookstores carrying our publications.

3752